A CANDLELIGHT ROMANCE

CANDLELIGHT ROMANCES

MAYBE TOMORROW

Marie Pershing

A CANDLELIGHT ROMANCE

To
Paul A. G_____, *M.D., physician and friend*
Jacque,
Helen,
et al.
and to
Steven, for Goldfisch

Published by
Dell Publishing Co., Inc.
1 Dag Hammarskjold Plaza
New York, New York 10017

Printed in the United States of America
First printing—March 1980

Chapter 1

Her ash-blonde head pressed against the glass, Jenna Wilson peered out the sixth-floor window of the tall building where the law firm of Hamilton, Redford and Jones had its offices.

"Need a ride home or do you have your car today?" one of the girls from the typing pool inquired pleasantly as she passed.

With the warm smile that made her the office favorite, Jenna shook her head. "Blake's picking me up, Elsa. He's just running late again, I guess. Thank you anyway."

It would have been nice if her brother had been on time, Jenna reflected. Fridays were always such a mad rush, and tonight was the spring play at the local junior college. She'd promised their young cousin Peta, who had second lead, that she'd be there to applaud. But if Blake didn't come soon—

Ten more minutes, Jenna told herself. And if Blake hadn't come by then, she'd better leave and catch a bus near Michigan Boulevard. Thank heavens, she had started dinner before she left for work that morning. It would take no time at all to toss a salad and reheat the leftover pie. She hoped Daphne would have remembered to put the casserole in the oven.

Jenna went back to her desk and carefully checked the Monday appointments scheduled for Mr. Hamilton. Since the former senator's heart attack the year before, Jenna liked to be certain that the old gentleman had at least one quiet break every hour. With that matter settled to her satisfaction, she went back to

5

the window again. There was still no sign of her ancient blue VW.

Jenna pulled on her brown winter coat and reached for the beige wool head scarf beside her purse. She had bought a new green scarf just last payday, a soft green that matched her eyes. Daphne had seen it and rushed to the mirror, folding the soft wool over the riot of blonde angel curls that framed her pretty face and exclaiming about how perfect the color would be for her new spring suit.

Jenna smiled ruefully, remembering. It was the last she'd seen of her new scarf, but who could refuse Daphne anything? Her twenty-year-old sister was so beautiful, she thought without envy—a true golden blonde with natural curls, lovely blue eyes under arching dark brows, and glamour in every inch of her slender five-feet-six model's figure.

Their mother had died when Daphne was only ten and Blake fourteen. Fifteen-year-old Jenna had helped her grieving father hold the family together then, but five years later their father's unexpected death had left them orphaned and with very little money. Jenna had not returned to college for her senior year. Instead, she took over the responsibility of the whole household, working to put Blake through law school and helping her unhappy younger sister find herself.

It hadn't been an easy five years. Always there were too many bills and not enough money for everything that was needed. And Daphne especially had resented having to leave their attractive family home in suburban Evanston to move to the small Chicago apartment, where the sisters shared one of the two shabby bedrooms.

But now Blake was a graduate attorney serving his first year's clerkship in Judge Hampton's law office, and things should soon be better for all of them, Jenna thought.

It was true, of course, that Daphne was scarcely self-supporting yet. After only one semester of college she had announced that she was leaving school to become a model. It took time, however, to get established, Daphne explained again and again during the first year. It also took expensive clothes and weekly visits to the hairdresser.

Tying the serviceable beige scarf over her own straight hair, which she wore in a neat chignon at the nape, Jenna critically examined her very ordinary reflection in the small pop-up mirror mounted in the top drawer of her desk. She usually didn't bother much with makeup. She had decided some years back that there wasn't much point in it for her. Jenna was a sensible young person and honest enough to admit that when the looks were passed out in the Wilson family, her brother Blake and young Daphne had got the lot.

Besides, the scar that marred her right cheek was still embarrassingly noticeable years after her childhood accident with the sled.

Even her eyes, dark-fringed and of a rare shade of green, could never measure up to Daphne's gorgeous blue ones, she acknowledged and closed the drawer firmly. She was reaching for her handbag and gloves when she heard the outer office door open.

"You're working late." Parker Hamilton regarded his young private secretary with affection. "Or is Blake late in picking you up?"

Jenna greeted him quietly in her lovely voice. She studied his face and said gently, "You're tired, senator. Was it bad in court today?"

He watched her work the brown leather gloves down over her fingers and gather up her purse. Pity

7

about that scar, he mused for the hundredth time. Jenna would have been a damn good-looking girl otherwise. Plumper than the modern vogue perhaps, and she couldn't hold a candle to young Daphne, of course, but how many men would want to spend their lives with a selfish scatterbrain like the younger Wilson girl?

His wife admired Jenna, too, and Martha was a good judge of character.

"When are you coming over for dinner again?" he asked. "Martha told me just this morning that she was eager to see you soon."

Jenna laughed. "You're both such dears. You gave me this job when I was practically without experience; you've been my friends through some of the hardest times. You are good people, you and Martha. I can never tell you enough how much I've appreciated your friendship."

The old man chuckled. "Knowing young people like you is what keeps Martha and me young, Jenna. And I would never have brought you into this office if I hadn't had the utmost confidence that you could do the job better than anyone else. It was just a matter of time until you got your feet on the ground, anyway. You already knew a great deal of the vocabulary, growing up in an attorney's family as you did. And your father, my dear, was one of my oldest friends. A fine man, Blake Wilson. If his son turns out even half so fine . . ."

Jenna reached out and touched his hand without speaking, then waved good-bye and left the office, running to catch a down elevator to the main lobby.

She started out into the drizzle, gasping at the frenzied wind that almost took her breath away.

Until three o'clock it had been a lovely April day with the tender scent of spring in the air and little tufts of soft white clouds trailing across a clear blue heaven. An April day holding promises of white lilacs and yellow tulips and fragrant drifts of purple hyacinths like those she remembered in the garden of the Evanston house.

The rains had started about an hour ago, pouring out of a darkening sky on home-going crowds of weary shoppers and tired office workers. Tormented trees in the park along the boulevard bent now in the biting wind sweeping in off Lake Michigan, and the street lights made little circles of misty glow in the early dusk. Jenna hurried along, her coat collar up, loathing the feel of the cold rain that dribbled down her neck.

The wind whipped at Jenna's head scarf and the rain beat against her face and soaked her legs and shoes. Clutching her purse to shield her eyes, she hurried across an intersection toward her bus stop and reached the partial shelter of a block of shops.

Shops with an air of elegance . . . a costly jewelers, custom-made shoes, a perfumer's boutique—and Greensleeves.

Jenna ducked into the entrance of the famous dress shop and leaned against the door, catching her breath and dashing the rivulets of rain from her face.

That was when she saw the dress. It was springtime pink, with a tucked top, a softly gathered skirt, and full sleeves that cuffed just below the elbow. It was a love of a dress—an April beauty—a dress for dreaming. Jenna took one look and wanted it desperately.

Nothing else was displayed in Greensleeves's window. Just that one rose-bright dress, with its matching cashmere cardigan casually draped beside it against a background of moss-green velvet to which vivid travel posters of England's Salisbury Cathedral and the soaring Sir Walter Scott Memorial in Edinburgh were jauntily attached.

9

Jenna stared uncertainly at the window. There was no price visible, but never in a hundred years would a Greensleeves dress be anywhere at all within her budget. She looked at the dress once more, tore her eyes away, and moved out to brave the wind and rain again. Suddenly she turned back, opened the shop door, and stood dripping on the cushiony moss-green rug.

"Come in," the smartly clad saleswoman welcomed. "Rain water won't harm good carpeting." She regarded Jenna doubtfully. "I was about to close. Was it something for you?"

Jenna pulled off the dripping head scarf uncertainly. "I was just passing and—that pink dress in the window?"

The saleswoman hesitated. "I'm afraid our largest sizes are twelves—very occasionally a size fourteen. That dress in the window is a ten, I believe."

Jenna clasped her hands tightly. "Oh, well— No, even a fourteen wouldn't be my size. It's such a lovely color, though, isn't it? Sort of a wild-rose pink."

"It's a shade known as opera pink," the woman said gently.

"It caught my eye in the rain. Well, I'd better—"

"Wait a minute or two, the rain might ease." The woman vanished toward the back of the shop and reappeared a moment later with a thick towel and a plastic rain hood. "That head scarf of yours is too wet to wear right now. Here, loosen that old-fashioned bun and dry your hair, my dear. You are a drowned rabbit!"

Jenna thanked her, shyly rubbing her long hair dry while the older woman watched her with a thoughtful expression.

"The rain loosens my tongue," she commented wryly. "You will forgive me if I make a personal suggestion?

You should consider a frosting. Your hair has a lovely texture. If you had some streaks of light blonde around your face—about here—and if you were to have the length cut to just an inch above the shoulders, so, it would swing free. Very chic and quite flattering."

Jenna flushed. "You really think so?" she ventured doubtfully. "You see, there's this scar. And then there's the problem of my weight too. I always tell myself that maybe tomorrow I'll start to diet, but I've just never bothered—"

"Ah!" The woman pounced. "But you *should* bother. You have good bones, and you stand so beautifully tall. Your smile is lovely, child. Think about what I tell you: There are cosmetics to cover the scar, and a frosting would put light blonde highlights in your hair. You need a clever shaping and a really good cut.

"All this can be done for you, but the matter of your weight—ah, that can only be solved by you, my dear," she said bluntly. "Go home. Think about what I say. Shed twenty-five pounds and come back to Greensleeves for a pink frock."

She handed Jenna the rain hood and opened the shop door. "It is well we met. First the haircut and the frosting, yes? You are too pretty to hide yourself as you do," she scolded gently. "Come back and see me again. Show me what you have done for yourself."

Thirty minutes later Jenna stepped off the bus and ran in a drenching rain the half block home. Her VW was parked at the curb, she observed with some surprise as she entered the drab main hallway, checked the mailbox, and went up the steps to their own apartment door. She shut it quietly behind her, hearing the murmur of voices in the living room.

Blake came out to warn her while she pulled off her

11

soggy shoes in the tiny vestibule. "We have a guest for dinner. Mark Nelson and I've been discussing plans for an office together next year, and I persuaded him to stay."

Jenna shivered a little as he helped her off with the soaked brown coat. "Oh, but—"

"No problem," he told her airily. "I stopped at the butcher's myself on the way home. I had to take lamb chops, he had no steak left this late in the day." He reached for a coat hanger. "Good lord, but you're wet, Jenna. You should have taken a cab."

"Lamb chops! Blake, we can't afford expensive cuts like lamb chops," she whispered shakily.

He gave her an annoyed look. "Cool it, Jenna," he told her in a soft voice. "The butcher was perfectly willing to put them on your account. Don't worry, I'll settle it myself next week if it upsets you so much." He patted her cheek. "Come on, don't be mad," he coaxed. "You know this could be important for me. For all of us. You and Daphne, too."

Jenna gave him an exasperated look and walked in her stocking feet to greet their guest. She smiled sunnily at the young attorney, who was beaming starry-eyed at Daphne, then excused herself to go and change.

Later, when they were doing dishes together in the tiny kitchen, Daphne stole a puzzled glance at her sister. "You've been unusually quiet. Something wrong at the office, or are you still peeved at Blake about the chops? Weren't they heavenly, though? Have the casserole tomorrow night, Jenna. I didn't get home in time to put it in the oven, anyway."

She admired her reflection in the small mirror above the sink. "The agency's booked me for a two-week modeling job in one of the really posh dress shops starting Monday."

"Oh, that's marvelous news!" Jenna spun around and kissed her. "I'm so happy for you. This may be the big break you've been waiting for, honey."

Daphne's pretty mouth twisted. "It's only for a two-week spring showing. I'll not be able to do dishes, of course. My nails, you know," she warned. She went on quickly, "There won't be much money in it—real money, I mean—but I'll get some fabulous discounts on clothes."

Jenna gave her a considering look. "Don't get into debt again with bills you can't pay off yourself, Daphne," she said carefully. "Anyway, your wardrobe's mighty adequate right now, I'd say."

"*You'd* say," Daphne responded sulkily and hung up the dish towel to dry.

"Daphne?" Her sister called after her, hesitantly. "Daphne, wait a minute. How do you think I'd look with my hair worn shorter—up to here, about—and maybe if I had a frosting to give me some highlights around my face?" She held her breath, waiting.

The younger girl turned slowly back. "I wouldn't have thought you'd want to highlight your face at all. Not with that scar, Jenna," she remarked with unconscious cruelty.

"But there are cosmetics specially made to cover scars. I should have started using them way back, I suppose." Jenna's voice was anxious. "What about the hair length and the frosting?"

"You've met a man!" Daphne shrieked with laughter. "That's it, isn't it? A man?"

Jenna was so surprised that her mouth opened in a little oval. "No—no man. Truly. It was raining hard, you see, and Blake hadn't come, so I ducked into a little shop and a very, very nice saleslady told me . . ." Her voice trailed off in a sudden memory of Don Rowland, the new attorney in the firm.

13

Daphne interrupted scornfully. "Honestly, Jenna, you're a babe in the woods, for all your years. You believe anything that anyone tells you."

Her brows together in a little frown, Jenna protested, "Twenty-five's not ancient, you know. And I'd truly rather believe in people, believe they're honest in what they say, than always be suspecting everyone."

Daphne yawned. "What's all this talk about Blake and Mark Nelson starting an office together?"

Jenna smiled. "Mainly just talk. They couldn't afford it for some years yet, I'm sure." Her voice was anxious. "But you still haven't said what you think about a haircut. What do you think, really?"

Daphne looked her over slowly. It was hard to understand Jenna in this mood. "I think it would be all right," she agreed finally. "With some frosting to light up that drab ash-blonde." Her pretty face flooded with amusement. "I still think it's a man."

Jenna glanced at the clock. "Horrors! It's after eight. Well, if I hurry I can still get there before Peta's play is completely over. Want to come along?"

"No, John's coming over for me later. Besides, you'll have to swim if you're going out." Daphne's voice was peevish again. "I wanted the car tonight—after all, Blake's had it all day—but he had to take Mark home, he said. He won't be back for hours."

She turned her beautiful eyes on Jenna, who was standing very still. "I thought you knew they'd gone."

"No. No, I didn't."

Daphne shrugged.

The evening sped quietly away after Daphne and her date left for a movie. Jenna changed the three beds and sorted the laundry, mending a few pieces of lingerie and sewing a missing button on Blake's favorite Geoffrey Beene shirt. Blake bought expensive clothes;

keeping up a good appearance was vital for a beginning attorney, he said. Jenna made a mental note to keep an eye open for Marshall Field's next sale of men's socks. Her brother would soon be needing replacements.

When the week's laundry was neatly sorted into the three canvas bags for Blake's Saturday trip to the Laundromat, Jenna tidied the living room, fertilized and watered her small house plants, checked the kitchen cupboards before planning the meals for the next week, and made out the grocery shopping list. At ten she took her shower, leaving a small lamp burning in the living room for Daphne and Blake, and decided to go to bed.

While she brushed out her hair and tied it back with a ribbon, she thought about the Greensleeves saleslady. What was it she had said? *You are too pretty to hide yourself as you do.*

Pretty? Jenna stared at her reflection in the dressing-table mirror. The green eyes stared doubtfully back.

She turned down the covers of Daphne's bed, propped herself up in her own, and reached for her knitting bag.

Daphne had a birthday next month, her twenty-first, and Jenna was making her a surprise—a knubby-knit shorty coat in a beautiful coral mohair yarn. She settled her needles and held up the nearly completed garment for a moment, loving the vibrant hue. It was a color she herself would never dare to wear, but on Daphne's slender figure it would be a stunning shaft of sunset.

Jenna let the knitting rest gently in her lap and put her head back. It had been a difficult day, and she was tired. Disappointed, too, she admitted. She was going to have to speak to Blake about the car and she dreaded fusses.

15

Frowning, she scooped yarn and needles into the knitting bag and thrust it from sight beneath her bed. The light out, she lay back thinking.

She resolved to buy a large kitchen calendar and post on it all the times when she would want her car. That was the businesslike way to handle the problem, she decided. It might be a good idea, too, if she used the calendar to jot down the various household tasks they had all agreed to share last year, when a bout of pneumonia had kept her two weeks in bed.

Blake had agreed then to take over the Saturday trip to the nearby Laundromat and to do the week's main shopping at the big supermarket. Daphne was to do the vacuuming, dusting, and assist with other housework. Jenna would continue to plan the meals, cook, help with the dishes, and pick up occasional necessities at the store.

It had been a good idea, portioning out the main jobs and sharing expenses, or it had seemed so at the time. But it wasn't working. At least not steadily enough to have settled down into routine. With each of them so busy it was easy to forget house chores, and Jenna refused to nag.

Well, she muttered to herself, she'd try the calendar idea.

She thumped the pillow into a more comfortable position and watched the flicker of light from an outside street light shine through a crack in the window shade to touch a large colored photograph of Abbotsford, Sir Walter Scott's well-loved Tweed Valley manor house, that hung on the wall beside her bed. The picture had belonged to her father. Scott was his favorite author, and Jenna had been reading the *Fair Maid of Perth* to him just before his death. Someday, she had promised him during his brief illness, she

16

would visit Scott's home and touch the stone walls of Scott's beloved Abbotsford.

Tears welled up in her eyes. It was hard enough to pay day-to-day bills, much less try to save for a trip to Scotland! She slipped out of bed, hastily adjusted the window shade, and flung herself back on the tumbled sheets. She would go quite out of her mind if she began to worry about money now, she reminded herself angrily.

After a little while she blew her nose, wiped the tears from her cheeks, thumped her pillow once more, and eventually went to sleep.

It was almost another week before Jenna found the courage to call her sister's beauty salon for an evening appointment. Friday was the best time for her, she told them, for then she'd have the whole weekend to get used to no "bun on the back of her neck" as Daphne was wont to describe her chignon.

Two hours later the hairdresser handed her a mirror. "It's quite a change. The shaping is excellent, but the frosting really did the trick."

Jenna fought a strong urge to burst into tears. "I'm afraid to look. What if I don't like it?"

"You'll like it. You look very chic."

Jenna steeled herself and seized the mirror. She raised astonished green eyes to the operator's. "Why, I *do* like it. I like it immensely! I don't look like me . . ."

Driving home, Jenna kept touching the springy ends of her hair. It felt so good. She skipped up the apartment steps with a light heart, eager to show Blake.

Her brother, however, was out of patience, for he had been waiting thirty minutes for the car. Jenna lent him the ten dollars he said he needed for the evening and invited his comments.

17

Blake looked at her and frowned. "I hope it didn't cost you anything," he said. "I could have cut it for you free."

Jenna swelled with indignation. Then she saw his eyes with the laughter in them.

"You look great," Blake said more seriously.

Jenna brightened. "But do you *like* it? I had a frosting, too."

He dropped a kiss on her cheek. "Yes, I like the haircut—can't see anything else different, though." He jiggled the car keys. "Thanks for the ten bucks, Jenna. Pay you back next week."

Daphne's comments when she came in from a dinner date were succinct. "That's more like it," she pronounced. "You don't look as if you're edging fifty anymore. Now for heaven's sake get yourself some new clothes for the office. Not brown!"

Her voice was charged with amusement; the blue eyes challenged. "Ready to tell me the man's name yet?"

Jenna found herself unable to look away.

"Let me see," Daphne mused. "Hamilton's married. Too old anyway. Redford? Never! Jones is dead. Jimmie Peterson doesn't know another female exists now that he's engaged. Calvin Fuller's at least two inches shorter than your five-seven. Ah, I have it—Jones's grandson's there now, isn't he? Came over from Detroit a month ago, Blake said."

Her lovely mouth curved in a smile. "I haven't met him yet. What's his name? Rowland something, isn't it?"

"What rubbish!" Jenna burst out sharply. "If you mean Don Rowland, he's old Mr. Jones's grandnephew. The man doesn't even know I exist."

"Good . . . then you've got a fresh start for Monday morning."

18

"Please—" Jenna's voice was unsteady, and she turned awkwardly away.

Daphne said slowly, "Sorry." Then, "I need to borrow some money. Can you lend me twenty dollars until payday?"

There was an awkward silence. Jenna murmured uneasily, "I thought you got paid today?"

"I get so damn sick of being poor!" Daphne's fingers drummed impatiently on the kitchen table. "Yes, of course, today was payday. Or would have been. I had some clothes put away for me. Jenna, Greensleeves gave me seventy percent off on some of the things I modeled. It's a sin to miss an opportunity like that."

Greensleeves! Jenna stared at her sister. "But that's a terribly expensive shop."

"I need expensive clothes, Jenna. At least some— It's like rolling a snowball downhill. I'll get more assignments if I dress the part. It's cumulative, don't you understand?"

"Did you get a pink dress?" Jenna's voice sounded tired now.

"Pink?" Daphne looked at her strangely. "There was a pink one, opera pink they said it was. Big in the waist, but they pinned it in okay. I wanted it. You could have fixed it for me easily, Jenna, but Madame said no. She was saving it for someone."

Jenna moved away to the window and stood looking out. "I'll have to write a check. There's only enough in my purse for tomorrow's groceries."

"A check's fine," Daphne cut in quickly.

Jenna nodded. Groceries—settling the bill with the butcher—the May rent—the gas bill—she was going to run short again this month. She thought shakily that Abbotsford would have to wait just that much longer, but thank God for her small savings account.

She remembered then how much the hairdresser had

just cost and wondered uneasily if she had been foolish, spending forty dollars and the rent yet to be paid.

As she had planned, Jenna was the first one at work on Monday. Blake dropped her off at the building entrance, still grumbling about having been awakened at dawn or just as bad, and Jenna let herself into the silent main office with her key and flicked on the light switches.

Her desk was in a quiet alcove adjoining Mr. Hamilton's private domain. She checked her daybook to refresh her memory about the senator's appointments for the week and her own few social obligations, and made a note to herself to cancel his luncheon meeting Wednesday because he would be in the state capital with the governor that day.

She filled the little Waterford vase with water for the single yellow tulip that Blake had brought home on Saturday from the supermarket, nervously checked her hair, added a light touch of lipstick, and was efficiently typing the first letter of the day when some of the girls from the typing pool came in.

Elsa Hamperdinch was on her way to the watercooler. A moment later a small shriek rang out. "It's marvelous! Simply marvelous! Turn around, let me see the back."

"I'll tell you something," Jenna threatened weakly. "Another scream like that and I leave for the day. I'm nervous enough as it is." She appealed, "You do like it?"

"I'll say I do. Wait—" Elsa brought Jennie and Katherine over to admire. Then Mr. Redford's secretary, Mrs. Babcock—who was fifty-five at least and rather distant—heard their excited voices and came across, too, looking Jenna over with a faint smile and then astonishing every one of them by observing

20

warmly, "It couldn't be more attractive, and I'm so glad you found the courage, my dear."

Shortly after that the day began, and it was a busy one, as Mondays always were.

Mr. Redford was in court, but he wouldn't have noticed her anyway, Jenna knew. Mr. Redford tended to look through, rather than at, a person. And Daphne was correct about Jim Peterson—Jim hardly noticed any girl at all lately.

On her way to take dictation Jenna passed Calvin Fuller. He raised his eyebrows and gave a soft, low whistle, and Jenna astonished both herself and the young man by winking back at him.

Mr. Hamilton began dictating as soon as she had seated herself. When he paused, thinking through a difficult phrase, Jenna looked up, and Parker Hamilton, who had known her since she was in kindergarten, had a puzzled look on his face.

"Jennifer Anne Wilson, you've cut your hair."

Jenna bit her lip worriedly. "Yes. Last Friday. Will it do?"

"It's very attractive, indeed. Martha will be pleased," he assured her and began to dictate again, smiling a little as he spoke. Martha was going to be delighted when he told her this tonight.

There was an abrupt rap on the door, and Don Rowland's confident voice said, "Good morning, sir." Then, seeing Jenna, added an automatic, "Miss Wilson."

He wanted to consult the older attorney for a few minutes about something that had occurred in court that morning, he said. To give them privacy Jenna started to leave, but Mr. Hamilton asked her to remain. "Miss Wilson is my right hand," he explained.

The younger man looked at Jenna, and then he looked again, and she could see the expression in his

21

eyes change. A pulse began to beat in her throat and she wished, wildly, that she was anywhere but there with him looking at her so intently.

He stopped at her desk later in the morning. "Miss Wilson," he said, laughing at her confusion, his light blue eyes watchful, "you and I must really get to know each other. Old Hamilton sings your praises so enthusiastically."

In the alcove light his skin seemed darkly suntanned. His light brown hair was modishly cut, and he looked very handsome in his well-tailored dark blue suit. It occurred to Jenna, however, that Don Rowland would probably look good in anything he wore, old blue jeans or country tweeds.

He bent closer to her. "Lunch with me, Jenna? There are things I want to discover."

"Things . . . to discover?"

His eyes made promises that sent her heart beating madly. "Well?" he asked.

"I can't. Not today," she answered softly. "I'm going with Mr. Hamilton to the Union Club to take notes for a Harvard alumni fund-raising luncheon meeting for him."

Donald Rowland's eyes darkened. "Tomorrow?" he asked.

"Tomorrow," she promised.

Chapter 2

When Jenna arrived for work in the morning, Don Rowland was leaning on the edge of her alcove desk, teasing Elsa, making Jeannie blush, even bringing a faint smile to Mrs. Babcock's reserved countenance.

"You're late," he said softly, watching her put away her things and open her daybook.

Elsa and Jeannie melted away, back to their desks in the outer office. Jenna felt a surge of happiness and said, a little breathlessly, "I had to catch a bus. Isn't it a lovely morning?"

"It is now." His light blue eyes held amusement. "Lunch with me today? Main entrance, twelve o'clock?"

She smiled back at him. "I'd like that. Thank you."

Just before noon she slipped away to brush her hair. She wasn't used it it yet, but she loved the way it fell, loose and free, to just above her shoulders.

Mrs. Babcock commented, "I surely do like your new hairdo. Have a pleasant time at lunch now, and don't worry if you run over a little. I brought a sandwich from home today, and I'll wait until you're back."

Jenna stood just inside the main entrance of the building, watching for him, and then she saw the sleek white Firebird double-parked at the curb. When Don waved to her, she hurried out.

He leaned over and opened the door. "Where would you like to go?" he asked.

She thought they would probably walk up to Michigan Boulevard, finding someplace rather nearby. "I only have an hour," she reminded him anxiously.

"But we're celebrating," he said quickly. "Our first date." He saw her worried face and laughed a little, and reached over and touched her hand. "The world won't cave in if you take an extra half hour, will it?"

She felt uncomfortable because she did not know if he was teasing her or not. She had had so little experience with this sort of thing. "I really think—" she began.

He had a charming smile. "Not quite what I intended," he told her a few minutes later in the busy coffee shop of the Palmer House. "There should be an orchestra playing, a quiet table for two in some secluded rendezvous."

He leaned across and caught her hand. "What are you doing tonight?"

Jenna hesitated. She was having an early dinner with Martha Hamilton, and then they were going to the Carteret Museum. The senator was leaving for Springfield, for he had an appointment with the governor on Wednesday. She and Martha had planned to spend the evening together, volunteering three hours of time to the collection of antique furniture in the Winsted Room.

"I'm having dinner with a friend." Caught up in happiness, Jenna broke her own rule of never discussing her friendship with the Hamiltons with anyone from the office. But this was different, this wasn't one of the staff. This was Don.

"When the senator's out of town, I often have dinner with his wife. We're old friends—I mean, they've known me forever." She smiled at him over the top of her coffee cup. "We polish furniture, antique furniture, at a museum sometimes. That's what I'm doing tonight."

"Good lord!"

"As volunteer workers," she added hastily. "Mrs. Hamilton's on the Board."

The girl was almost pretty when she was all excited like that, he thought, watching the rose color touch her face. "It sounds a bit of a bore."

She wished wistfully that he would suggest another evening. She asked, "How do you like Chicago now that you've been here a month?"

Chicago was going to turn out very well indeed for him, he confided. Detroit had had all the appearances

24

of a dead end, unfortunately. "You have to know the right people, the 'in' group, to get ahead in Detroit," he explained blandly. "In Chicago too, of course, only my chances are rather good here. I pulled a few choice strings and my great-aunt by marriage, Bedford Jones's widow, got me right into the Hamilton setup."

He was, she supposed, an ambitious man. And what was wrong with that? It was ridiculous to feel let down like this because of what he had said. She stirred uneasily and looked down at her watch. "I really must be getting back," she said.

The Firebird slid into the five-minute parking slot in front of their building. Jenna put one hand on the car door. "Thank you. I enjoyed it very much." Her voice sounded cool and somewhat aloof.

"Now that's Miss Wilson talking," Don murmured, studying her face. Something he had said back in the coffee shop had disturbed her and he wondered what it was. Jenna was an old-fashioned kind of girl—he'd have to watch himself.

"How does my darling Jenna say thank you?" He paused significantly.

She blushed, and he bent his head and kissed her cheek lightly. "Are you going straight to the Hamiltons from work? May I drop you off there?"

"It's way up in Lake Forest," she warned him.

"Good." He laughed softly. "I wish it were even farther, but at least I'll have that much of you."

Her world slid back into happy focus. She smiled shyly at him and thanked him once more for her lunch.

He said, "Five fifteen? Main entrance?" Rather well pleased with himself he drove off to garage the car. The quick look into Jenna's daybook early that morning had been a damn good idea. He had a list of every

Hamilton appointment—social and professional—for the next four weeks.

The afternoon hours slid by while Jenna typed the senator's Harvard report and the last of his letters. Then she took dictation from Mr. Redford so that Mrs. Babcock could leave early and get to her dental appointment.

She was glad to be busy. When she had transcribed her notes for Mrs. Babcock, the clock said ten after five.

The magic of loving had changed her life so completely. Any minute now she could leave and run to meet Don. She found she was smiling, just thinking of him. Of his light brown hair—his blue eyes—the urbane ease with which he moved—

The Firebird was there at five fifteen, double-parked, and Don lounged at the wheel, waiting for her. She ran forward, her blonde hair swinging at her shoulders, and climbed in. "I'm not late, am I? Have you been waiting long?"

The car moved effortlessly away from the curb and into the flow of traffic. "Not long. You're prompt, Miss Wilson, for a girl."

She was beginning to feel more at ease with him. "Hm . . . that sounds as if you've known a good many," she said.

"Not really. Not intimately, that is."

She colored at that, and he laughed delightedly. "Ah, my darling Miss Wilson, what did you expect with that retort? But now I've met you and things will be different."

Something at the back of her mind tried to be heard. She thought fleetingly of the month he'd been there in the office, scarcely giving her the time of day, but she shrugged the warning voice impatiently away.

This was *now* and they were together, driving in an exciting car—and life seemed very, very good.

"We'll take 14 and 41 to Sheridan Road, then stop for a few minutes at my club in Kenilworth," Don said. He turned momentarily toward her. "Got your date book handy in your purse? I want to fix up a few evenings before you get all booked."

She glanced at him. "Well, no, I don't—"

He challenged her, "Do you mean to tell me you don't have one of those little calendar date books in your handbag? A pretty girl like you?"

Jenna admitted honestly, "There haven't been all that many—dates, I mean—and I just, well, I just keep a record of them in my office daybook. It's convenient that way."

"For the record," he stated firmly, "I'm officially asking if you're free this Friday."

She caught her breath. What miserable bad luck had made her promise Peta— "I can't," she said. "I'm sorry, Don."

"Then Saturday?" he asked smoothly. "Is Saturday free? I thought we might drive out in the country in the late afternoon, have dinner somewhere near Lake Geneva, and see if spring's arrived."

She was crushed. "Don, I'm having dinner with the Hamiltons. Their fiftieth wedding anniversary is coming up, and I'm helping organize some of the arrangements for them." She reached out her hand and touched his sleeve. "Maybe I could postpone it—I could call and ask. Would you want me to do that? Martha'd understand."

So she called Mrs. Hamilton "Martha." "No, don't do that," he said quickly. "I want you to keep your promises, Jenna. That's part of the sweetness of you."

With tenderness in his voice he said, "It seems that

27

you and I are going to have to be content with luncheon dates for a while, darling Jenna."

She offered shyly, "I have nothing planned for Sunday, Don. Would you like to come over for dinner with us? My sister won't be there, but Blake, my brother, would enjoy meeting you. He's an attorney too."

Regretfully, he explained that Sunday was out. He'd had an appointment for several weeks and couldn't back out now. His eyes narrowed in thought, photographically recalling her daybook calendar for the following week.

They turned into the private drive of the Thunder Bay Country Club and pulled up under the covered entrance. "Tie a little string around your finger, Jenna," Don said, nodding to the car-park attendant. "Saturday of the next week's all mine."

Jenna swallowed hard. "I'm jinxed," she admitted, taking his hand and walking with him into the lounge.

"Why is that?" he asked casually, forcing her to explain. He steered her into the bar. "If you're going to say you're booked for next Saturday too, at least let me have a martini in my hand when you tell me."

She could have wept. "White wine, please," she told the red-haired waitress who had come at once to their table. She turned to Don. "You're going to hate me when I tell you, but next Saturday is the Hamiltons' anniversary party. At the North Shore Club. A big affair—a reception, dinner, dancing. Oh, heaps of VIPs, Don, senators he used to work with, one member of the Supreme Court, people from Chicago, Palm Beach, Palm Springs, and oh, everywhere, I guess. I have to be there, Don. They're counting on me."

He demanded to know, "All week and weekends too?"

"No, it's not like that at all, Don. Please understand." She felt tears sting her eyes and forced them back. "I've known them since I was a little girl. They have no children of their own, you know. I was even invited to Washington to accompany them to a Presidential Inaugural Ball."

She smiled as she remembered. "I'm helping them with the arrangements, true—but I'll be at their party as a guest, not part of the hired help. You don't have to be offended for me, Don, but it's sweet of you to worry."

He stared moodily at her, and his fingers twirled the martini glass around and around. "Small comfort . . . I'll be picturing you there, looking like a dream in your long frock, your chosen escort at your side among all those illustrious dinner guests, then holding you in his arms for the dancing."

She fought down a giggle that almost broke free as she thought of her five-year-old beige formal. "Well, not quite like that," she said, for she could see the tense, white line around his lips. "My dress is old, and I haven't an escort—not a proper one, that is, although there are always a number of men who come alone to parties like that, for one reason or another, and the Hamiltons see to it that I'm taken care of."

He said bitterly, "It seems a pity. We want to be together but we can't. You'll be at the Hamilton affair, and I'll be all alone at home."

Hesitantly, she asked, "Would you like to come, Don? I mean, if I could get you an invitation?"

He frowned. "If you asked Mrs. Hamilton to allow you to bring your own escort, do you think she might agree?"

"Of course she would. She'd be delighted. They're always—well, they'll be delighted, both of them." She smiled gently at him, for he suddenly looked so pleased. "I'll ask Martha tonight; that's what I'll do."

Mr. Hamilton was in court Thursday morning and returned to the office just before twelve. Jenna dashed around, finishing some office errands, and hurried back to her desk to find Don waiting there to take her out to lunch. They were going to drive up to Grant Park and have a picnic box lunch in the springtime sunshine.

She did wonder, though, why Mr. Hamilton was frowning as he stood in the doorway of his office and watched them leave together. Perhaps it had been a bad time in court. The Jansen case was on his mind, she knew.

She was too happy to worry about anything for very long. Don had asked her to lunch six workdays in a row! He telephoned her in the evenings too, and his voice sent delightful little shivers up her spine.

"This Don," Daphne said one night. "Why don't you ever have a date with him?"

Jenna explained about the crowded two-week calendar, laughing now about it with her sister. "He's taking me to the Hamilton party on Saturday, though," she added. "Martha sent him an invitation."

"You ought to get a new dress. That old beige!" Daphne said. "When will Blake and I get to meet this paragon, then? On Saturday?"

"Well, no," Jenna said. "Not Saturday." He was going to meet her at the North Shore Club because she'd be there early to help Martha. She wasn't too eager to introduce Don to Daphne yet. Later, when she was used to being happy, she knew she'd feel different about that. But not yet. Not yet for a while.

The next Friday after work she was near Michigan Boulevard, walking up to catch a bus and feeling blissfully content, what with May sunshine and a new beau and a wonderful party the next day.

"I really should stop," she said to herself. Greensleeves was just up ahead one block.

Greensleeves had just finished a showing. Twenty delicate gilt chairs stood in a double semicircle, and one model was still in a wedding frock when Jenna came hesitantly in. She looked from one face to another, hoping to see her friend.

She tried to describe her. "Not quite as tall as I am—very slender—dark hair beautifully styled, worn up like this at the sides."

A little smile touched the lips of the saleslady who had approached her. "That would be Madame. Madame Green. None other. She's just returned from her dress salon in Paris, and I'm afraid she's not here right now. Would you like to leave a message for her?"

"Are you saying she owns Greensleeves?" Jenna asked, astonished. "But she was so sweet to me . . . I had no idea. Yes, please, if you would be so kind, give her this message from me. Tell her I had my hair done exactly as she suggested. It cost me forty dollars and it was worth every penny of it. Tell her I'm working on the weight now, and I'll stop in again and see her. Would you tell her all that?" she asked.

"Every word," promised the woman.

It was with real despair that Jenna awakened Sunday morning, feeling feverish and almost certain that she was getting a sore throat. A cold! How beastly to have this happen after such a heavenly party!

She swallowed two aspirins, thought briefly about a cup of hot tea, but changed her mind and hurried back to bed.

"What's wrong?" Daphne asked, peering at her from the other bed.

31

"A cold, I guess. I feel wretched. I hope I didn't give it to Don last night."

"Have a good time?"

Jenna closed her eyes. "Heavenly. Oh, a marvelous dinner—that French chef, you know. Don had a great time. He's really a nice person, Daphne . . . sensitive about other people's feelings. He was pleasant even to the stuffiest ones. Lots of young people wouldn't want to miss a single dance, but he sat and chatted with that old Supreme Court Justice, so he wouldn't feel left out when nearly everyone else was dancing."

"Better stop talking," Daphne suggested. "Your voice is hoarse."

Jenna's cold was only a little better on Monday, and with her past history of pneumonia the better part of valor was to stay home from work and take care of herself.

"I'll miss you so much," she said wistfully when Don called.

If she had to be sick, he sympathized, she'd picked a good day because he was having lunch with the Justice and wouldn't have been able to see her at noon anyway. "I'm terribly grateful to you, Jenna," he said. "Contacts like that are invaluable to a young man on his way up."

She thought about that for much of the day. She felt a little unhappy and wasn't at all sure why, and finally attributed her low spirits to the cold itself.

That evening Don came to the apartment. Mr. Hamilton had a report he wanted Jenna to read before work tomorrow, and he had asked Mrs. Babcock if she could drop it off to Jenna on her way home. Mrs. Babcock had been delighted to oblige, but then, at the very last moment, her nephew had called from the airport and asked her to come out to O'Hare and have dinner with him between planes. Mrs. Babcock had thought of Mr. Rowland right away, and Don had said of course he'd be glad to bring it out to Jenna. He had wanted to see her anyway.

Jenna got up to greet him, feeling much better but looking rather peaked in her old blue robe. "I'll be in to work tomorrow," she assured him. She wouldn't let him get close at all, however, for she didn't want him to catch her cold.

Daphne laughed at that and said, "How about last Saturday night?" But she insisted, nevertheless, that Jenna ought to get back to bed.

Later she came in to see if her sister needed anything. She sat on the edge of her own bed and watched Jenna, who was reading the report and making penciled notes to Mr. Hamilton in the margins.

"He's nice," Daphne remarked rather quietly for Daphne. "Just as you said."

Jenna looked at her. "You're awfully quiet. Are you catching my cold?"

She was glad she felt well enough to go back to work on Tuesday. Daphne was in such a miserable mood that it was wonderful to escape from the apartment.

Don was in a bad mood all week too. Jenna grew pensive, wondering what ailed everybody.

"Spring fever?" Mrs. Babcock suggested helpfully. "It affects different people in different ways."

By Friday Jenna had fretted herself into a migraine headache. Blake picked her up at work just before noon and took her home early, and she thought sadly, "I never even had a chance to say hello to Don today."

Rest and quiet and a special tablet from the physician brought relief, but when Daphne came in at nine o'clock that night, there was no meal prepared for her. Quite out of sorts, Daphne pranced into the kitchen and began to make an omelet.

Blake was out, and Jenna slept until the doorbell roused her. She lay quietly, her eyes on the picture of

Abbotsford House, wondering who it was so late in the evening. From the kitchen came Daphne's exasperated exclamation, then her high heels clicked across the hallway to the front door.

Jenna heard a man's voice, then her sister's lilting laughter. She raised her head, listening. It was Don! Don had come to see her.

Joyfully, she got to her feet. She felt better. Much better. She brushed her hair and slipped into a fresh white blouse.

Strange that Daphne hadn't come to tell her she had a caller, but they were probably chatting a bit first. Don was always an amusing companion. Jenna pushed the bedroom door ajar so that her sister would know she was awake, and went back to the mirror to finish the makeup of her face.

She wasn't really listening, not in the least way trying to overhear, but with the bedroom door open, their voices sounded very clear coming down the darkened corridor from the living room.

Jenna frowned, staring into the mirror with unseeing eyes. Don was saying, " . . . Can't get you out of my mind . . . since Monday, nothing else . . . met you at last, banal as that sounds—"

And Daphne's soft-voiced reply, "You're Jenna's . . . hurt my sister . . ."

"I'm not in love with her. We're only friends."

Jenna sank down on the bed. Faintness swept over her in nauseating waves.

Down the corridor came Daphne's muted voice. ". . . Not what she thinks."

"I can't help what she thinks. I never told her I loved her. Daphne, have a heart—she's at least thirty pounds overweight. And that scar!" He groaned. "Oh, angel, I'm not always a nice person; you may as well know that. I planned to use her—or try to, she's a wily one—because she's got such good connections with old man Hamilton. But it took just one look at you and— Angel, you're beautiful . . . "

There was silence in the living room.

The color had all drained out of Jenna's face. She felt torn in two: half of her yearned to scream and tear down walls, but the other half wanted only to creep under the bedcovers and close her eyes and die. Die of grief and damaged pride and blasted dreams . . .

But it was too late for that. Daphne, her golden curls awry, stood there in the doorway, seeing the suffering on her sister's face.

"Oh, my God," Daphne breathed. "You're awake. You heard us?"

Jenna turned back to the mirror and shakily redid her face. She said, "Please go. I'd like to be alone."

Daphne stepped gingerly into the room. "You weren't supposed to hear the news that way. I'm sorry about that, really I am, but it's just as well you know. Don and I fell in love, just like that. It's nobody's fault. Please don't hate us."

Jenna was crumbling apart inside herself. "I don't hate you. Go back to him, Daphne. If you're both in love, I'll give you my blessing just like in an old-fashioned novel. But you can tell Don—"

She reached for her handbag and groped for the car keys within. "—Tell Don it's the—the—the other things I'll find hard to forgive."

Daphne stood there with her mouth open. "You're not going out, are you? It's late, and you've had a headache all day. Are you crazy? Don! Don, come and talk to her—"

Jenna flashed down the hall, flung open the door, and ran down the stairs to the little blue VW parked in a puddle by the curb. She drove for forty minutes, heading west.

She thought sadly, so that was how a dream ended. Heartbreak welled up inside her, mingling with the bitter feeling of shame and broken pride.

She had been a fool, an utter fool, to think that Don had been attracted to her. From the very first time he had noticed her, that morning in Parker Hamilton's office, it had been only her close association with the senator that had interested Don Rowland. He had hoped to capitalize on her friendship with the socially prominent Hamiltons to further his own career.

Sick with humiliation, she knew that was true.

The hurt was deep. And it did not help her heartbreak to realize that she was only one of countless stepping-stones the young attorney would make use of throughout his lifetime.

The senator was no fool. He had tried to warn her about Don, she realized that now. Her face flushed as she remembered his hesitant voice expressing concern regarding people who were, as he termed them, heartless opportunists. She had felt uncomfortable under Mr. Hamilton's troubled gaze. Well, now she knew why—

A tear spilled down her cheek. It was her fault—all of it. She had been too eager to be happy. All too willing to be captivated by Don's lighthearted gallantries—

With a shaking hand she swept the tears from her cheeks. It would be no comfort to cry. Besides, she told herself sharply, it was dangerous when one was driving.

Raindrops spattered against the car. Jenna switched on the windshield wipers and automatically dropped her speed. Some distance ahead glimmered the red taillights of the station wagon that had passed with a small child waving to her from the back.

The highway had divided into four lanes separated

by a narrow grassy verge, and signs indicated that they were approaching an intersection with a state road. Jenna began to look for an appropriate place to turn. It must be close to midnight, she thought, and the rain was almost over. It was time to go home.

Half a mile ahead she saw the bright headlights of a car approaching from the opposite direction, coming fast and weaving erratically. Jenna became tense and slowed down, edging far over into the right-hand lane. The car ahead of her was slowing down too; she saw the flare of its brake lights.

Even as she watched, the weaving car hurtled across the median and skidded on the slippery pavement, slammed into the first vehicle with a frightful sound of tearing metal, glanced off, and came straight at Jenna.

The noise of the crash echoed in her ears as she shot forward against her seat belt.

Working her way through misty layers of consciousness, Jenna heard whimpering near her head. She opened her eyes and the little whimpers ceased.

The night was silent again. Sudden memory flooded back. Her side hurt, yet she felt strangely numb. She raised her hand and brushed at the fragments of glass that seemed to have disintegrated over her face and hair. She felt a wet stickiness on her fingers. Miraculously her headlights still beamed. She reached forward to be certain that the ignition was off. Moving slowly now, she groped for her handbag and found the little flashlight within it.

The door on her side would not open, and Jenna, clutching the flashlight, moved across the front seat and half-slid, half-fell from the car onto the shoulder of the road. Fighting nausea, she closed her eyes for a moment.

Somewhere in the darkness behind her was the wreck of the car that had caused the accident. Jenna wasted no time looking. She staggered to the grassy median strip where she could see the twisted steel that had been a white station wagon only minutes before.

A door had been flung open and a woman hung half out of what had been the front seat. Jenna saw the dreadful gash on her left arm. "Got to get you out. If I help you, can you move a little?" she asked, dragging the moaning woman as best she could to the safety of the grass behind them. Jenna was desperate. Perhaps they shouldn't be moved, but she smelled gasoline, and surely . . .

Searching for the child, she flashed her light frantically into the rear area of the wrecked car. In the back seat she saw a small arm in a scarlet sweater.

The odor of gasoline was stronger. She reached in through the jagged spears of glass in the broken window, wrenched open the door, and nearly fainted with the scalding pain. Willing herself not to lose consciousness, she leaned against the wreck, panting for breath.

There was a squeal of brakes—light from a powerful flashlight—a man's decisive voice shouting orders to the driver of another car to get help—

"Here!" Jenna called out hoarsely. "Help me here."

A tall, dark-haired man carrying a black bag ran toward her. He saw her white face, blood-matted hair, and torn blouse. "My God!"

"The child—"

"I'm a doctor," he said curtly. "Let me see your head."

"It's nothing. Get the child out—can't you smell the gasoline?" She was frantic, her green eyes huge with pain.

He reached into the wreckage and lifted out a little boy, swiftly carrying him in his arms to a safe distance.

He raced back to seize her and guide her to safety near the child.

Jenna was very short of breath now. "Scalp wounds . . . bleed freely . . . that's in . . . my first-aid book," she muttered incoherently. "Chest hurts," she whimpered.

The tall man had carried the unconscious woman to lie beside the boy. He hastily bound up the woman's arm to stop the hemorrhaging, shrugged off his coat, and covered the two of them, bending down to check the child's pulse. "Both alive. Now you."

He reached down for his bag.

Jenna staggered to her feet. "Hurts . . . to breathe," she whispered, hearing police sirens and ambulance alarms coming out of the night. There were many voices now and something was burning. Great flames leaped high.

She reached out for his hand, wanting the comfort of a human touch. Dr. Fraser caught her in his arms as she collapsed. There was a little bloody froth at the corner of her mouth.

She did not hear his terse directions to the ambulance men. "Here first! Emergency . . . respiratory distress!"

Chapter 3

Jenna awakened in pain, drawing agonizing breaths that thrust knifelike while she struggled to open her eyes. Above her was a flood of brilliant light. Masked faces bent over her; terse voices gave commands. She tried to speak, heard a sobbing groan and closed her eyes again, drifting down—down—down into a peaceful, pain-free place.

* * *

She opened her eyes and it was night. "Again—or still?" she asked weakly. Her head felt heavy . . . strange . . .

"Ah, there you are," a calm voice answered her. "Everything's just fine, Miss Wilson. How do you feel?" The nurse's face floated into view.

"My head. It's so heavy."

"That's because of the bump you got. It will feel better tomorrow. Rest now. You're going to be just fine."

Jenna sighed. "Again—or still?" she murmured once more and shut her eyes obediently.

She heard the nurse speak in low tones to someone else in the room. " . . . Dreaming, doctor."

A warm hand reached out and covered one of hers. "It's night again," a reassuring voice said, folding her fingers firmly within his own. "The accident was yesterday. Try to sleep. You're going to be all right, Jenna."

She begged him, "Don't go—it's burning—hurts so—"

There was the sound of quiet steps, the nurse's low murmur as she readied the injection. A man's response—

"Please—please—" Jenna moaned, opening her eyes.

He bent close over her. She could see dark eyes, dark brown hair, a wide smile. "You're a brave girl," he said. "A brave, brave girl."

"Who—?"

"I'm Simon."

Jenna fell asleep, holding his hand, feeling comforted and safe with him there.

When she awakened again, it was daylight and she was propped up against the pillows. She could smell hyacinths. Hyacinths and roses. She felt as if she were floating in a hazy cloud. The pain was gone, but she knew it was hiding in the farthest corner to come roaring back when she coughed.

She felt wretched. She moved her head sideways on the pillows and saw tubes and bottles and metal stands. One of the tubes seemed to be in her chest.

"Good morning." It was a young voice. A pretty girl in a white uniform was at the bedside. "I'm the medical technologist, and you'll be seeing a lot of me. I'll be in for blood samples." She smiled cheerfully, replacing Jenna's arm gently on the coverlet.

"Where's Simon?" Jenna asked through the cloudy haze.

"Simon who?"

"Don't you know? He was here." She closed her eyes and moved her head restlessly.

There were voices in the hallway, and a nurse came quietly in and reached for her pulse. "You're looking better today, Miss Wilson. Here's Dr. Randall to see you."

"You and I got acquainted the night the ambulance brought you in, but you won't remember me, young lady." The gray-haired man's voice was as friendly as his pleasant face. He spoke to the nurse in a low tone and orders were written on the clipboard she carried. Jenna heard scraps of them: " . . . So continue with the posterior intercostal nerve block . . . five cc's two percent procaine . . . eight-hour intervals until . . . want X rays every . . . the arterial blood gases measured serially . . . Penrose drain . . . "

Jenna lifted a weary hand. She interrupted them in a little rush of words. "Please—where am I?"

The gray-haired surgeon murmured something to the nurse. "You're in Augustana Hospital. Do you remember the accident?" he asked Jenna.

Green eyes flew wide. "That woman—the little boy—?"

Dr. Randall nodded approvingly. "Good. You've remembered. They owe you their lives, I hear. God knows how you did it with those broken ribs and developing pneumothorax." He reached down and patted her hand.

"Ribs? All this—is—ribs?"

He told her mildly, "And a few other things. But all under control, Miss Wilson. We're going to keep you very quiet for a week or so and let that lung heal."

He completed his careful examination. "Now then, nurse, I think we'll say no visitors—except the brother and sister briefly, toward the end of the week. And I want frequent checks on that cough reflex." Then to Jenna, "You're doing a splendid job of recovering, my dear, and we're going to see that you have a great deal of rest and no worries."

She had to ask. "The other car?"

He shook his head. His voice became very matter of fact. "I understand there was only the driver." He bid her good-bye then, saying in his calm voice that he would be seeing her again soon.

Jenna drifted off to sleep, wishing she had remembered to ask them about Simon.

The morning vanished in taking X rays, being turned in bed, and sponge baths. She remembered little of all this, for the nurses were quick and competent, and she drowsed in blissfully pain-free naps.

One afternoon Daphne came, bearing yellow tulips. "They said I could only stay five minutes, and you weren't to talk," she complained indignantly. "Don brought me in his Firebird, and they wouldn't even let him come up." She indicated the plant. "These are from Don and me."

Jenna winced and her heavy lashes fluttered briefly down.

"How are you?" Daphne asked, a shocked expression marring her prettiness. "I must say you look awful! Have you seen your face?"

Jenna shook her head mutely.

"And your hair snipped off in all those places!" Daphne reached for a mirror on the dresser, but a long arm shot out and seized it from her hand.

"No," said a firm voice.

Daphne whirled around, blue skirt flaring out about her lovely legs. She saw a tall, dark-haired man looking at her with a sardonic gleam in his brown eyes. A very handsome man in an expensively tailored dark gray suit . . .

Daphne gave him her devastating smile. "Who are you?" she asked, her blue eyes wide and innocent.

Jenna answered her. "That's Simon."

"Jenna, darling," Daphne said, "you do find the most delightful men. Simon who?"

A little red-haired nurse poked her head through the doorway. "Telephone, Dr. Fraser."

"Well!" observed Daphne when they were alone again. "He's one of the handsomest men I've ever seen." She looked thoughtfully at the red roses in the tall vase on the windowsill and strolled casually over to inspect the card. "Hmm . . . Martha and Parker Hamilton," she read. "Then who sent the white hyacinths?"

Jenna moved her head slightly in a weary "don't know" fashion. She felt terribly tired and her head had begun to ache. She wanted to sleep.

"I did." Dr. Fraser was back in the room again. "Your sister's a hyacinth-girl."

Daphne's blue eyes narrowed slightly.

43

"Leaving?" he asked smoothly. "May I have the pleasure of walking you to the elevator?"

He stood with his hands in his trouser pockets, jingling his change, while Daphne kissed her sister goodbye.

And that was that, Jenna reflected with a little sigh. One more conquest for Daphne. She closed her eyes.

"Sleepy?" he inquired softly, pulling a chair close to the bed. "They say 'no visitors' but I don't count."

The green eyes flew open. "Are you my physician?"

He shook his head and stared at her for a long moment. "A friend."

"She said—I looked dreadful. That's why—I wasn't to have a mirror—wasn't it?" she wanted to know.

He leaned over and took her cold hand in his warm one. "Can you wait a day or two?" he asked quietly. "Will you believe me if I tell you that it's only minor lacerations—plus one big bump?"

She held tightly to his large hand.

He continued, "If you're going to fuss and let her upset you, I'd rather you looked now, but if you could trust me—?"

Jenna felt as if she had been trusting him all her life. "You have no idea—how expensive—my hair was," she said weakly. "Forty dollars."

He looked mildly amazed.

"Don't go," she said sleepily. "You always—go away."

He told her, "I keep coming back."

When she awakened again, it was evening and Blake was there to see her. "Hello," she said, trying to sound very healthy.

Blake gave her a quick kiss and squeezed her hand hard. "How are you?" he asked in a subdued sort of voice, staring at all the complicated equipment of the water-seal drainage for reexpansion of her damaged

44

lung: the plastic catheter in her chest, and the rubber tubing and glass connector, the Penrose drain and the gallon jar half filled with aqueous Zephiran.

"Jenna," he said, "I'm worried sick—what *is* all this stuff? Are you going to be all right?"

Jenna reflected that that wasn't exactly the sort of thing one said to a hospital patient, but she knew it indicated how concerned her brother was. She made her voice cheerful, but it took so much energy to talk. "I'm going—to be fine. All the doctors—tell me so."

"You wrecked the car. And I mean really totaled it."

"Oh." Somehow she hadn't thought about the car at all. "Well—probably the insurance will—"

"That old VW? And a three-car accident? It'll be tied up in the courts for a year!"

Jenna felt herself begin to tremble. "Blake—I carry good auto insurance. And—Mr. Hamilton himself came up—yesterday, they tell me—to make sure—my medical insurance—took care of everything I—needed here. And the physicians, too. Blake, the bills—are all covered."

He got up restlessly and stood looking out the window. "You're going to have to get another car. Yours can't be fixed. It was old, anyway. He owes it to you, that nineteen-year-old creep that struck you. Drunk, I hear."

She shivered. "Blake, he's dead."

"His folks aren't. Did you know he was the son of the Pro-Gardner Company? The biggest construction outfit in the state of Illinois?"

Tears came flooding down her face. "Please, Blake—"

He was stricken. "Sorry, Jenna. Didn't mean to upset you. It just makes me so damn mad! Stop crying, will you? Oh lord, should I call someone?"

45

"I'm here," said a tightly controlled voice from the doorway.

Jenna called out faintly, "Simon—"

After that there were no visitors. Jenna obediently followed orders and slept and rested when she was told to do so and ate when meals arrived. The food tasted flat at first, and she found it difficult to finish even the small portions which she was served, but she was a good patient. They had told her that adequate nutrition was essential to hasten tissue repair within her lung.

She was X-rayed and examined and bathed, and they told her they were pleased with her progress. Mostly, she slept. Gradually the drowsiness which had pervaded the early days drifted away and she felt an interest in life again.

A pretty, dark-skinned nurses' aide gently brushed her hair into a semblance of its former style, crooning softly over the healing lacerations. "It is not bad now, no?" Miss Sanchez comforted, handing her a mirror.

Jenna peered at her reflection. "Yes—I mean—no," she told the tiny girl from Cuba. And it really wasn't too bad at all. She had been afraid, after Daphne's first visit, but it was exactly as Simon had said.

She missed Simon. He had not been in to see her for several days. Away on a brief trip, explained the card that had accompanied pink hyacinths from him.

Blake and Daphne visited her again, tiptoeing into the room and obviously under orders not to mention anything that would upset her. Jenna sighed with real relief when they left, their behavior had been so unnatural. On Wednesday the Hamiltons were allowed to see her briefly.

She felt better and, even though Mr. Hamilton had assured her that she must not concern herself about work, she began to worry about her job. And about

46

how long she would be in the hospital. Dr. Randall said she would have to stay approximately three weeks. He explained that inactivity for at least that long was necessary to assure reexpansion and lessen the likelihood of reopening the leak. That sounded rather ominous to her.

All this must be costing the earth, she fretted. Surgeons, physicians, consultations, special equipment, all those laboratory tests, and X rays—oh, dozens of X rays. And now the physical therapist who came to demonstrate breathing exercises!

One day she asked Blake how they were making out at home without her, and her brother looked grim and did not speak. Jenna worried about that too, and gave him the paycheck that Mr. Hamilton had very kindly brought along when he came to see her, warning him to be sure to take care of the rent first of all.

At least Daphne was her old self again, bubbling over with happiness. She and Don were in love. One evening they came together to the hospital and stood by her bed, holding hands and full of plans for the future.

Jenna was surprised how little she really cared.

The next afternoon she awakened from a nap and there was Simon again, smiling at her. Simon could tell her simply so she'd understand. She asked, "What happened to me—in the accident, I mean? Dr. Randall told me—I think—but I'm afraid I didn't listen, or didn't understand him. At least not then. All that tubing and the—what did you call it? The catheter inserted in my chest."

On impact she had hit the steering wheel with her chest and fractured several ribs, he told her quietly, holding her hand tightly, for she had begun to tremble a little. Her head had probably struck a window and she had multiple lacerations—none of them serious al-

47

though they had indeed bled freely, he added. Fortunately, she had been wearing her seat belt and was not ejected from the car. Perhaps when she pulled the injured woman to safety and located the child almost hidden from view in the wreck, wrenching open a door to reach him, a sharp end of the fractured ribs had torn her right lung. The resulting air leak had caused the lung to collapse.

"Your chart probably reads something like: A tension pneumothorax subsequent to laceration of right lung, subsequent to three fractured ribs. Intact thorax. Minor facial and scalp lacerations. Blow on head; no concussion."

She whispered, "That's why it hurt so dreadfully? Why I could scarcely breathe?"

"That's why."

He did not intend to tell her of the medical emergency that had threatened her life at that time, nor of the expedient measures he had been forced to employ at the scene of the accident before they could transport her. He had inserted a large-bore intravenous needle into the pleural cavity to begin aspirating the air present under pressure there, and then, applying oxygen, had ridden in the ambulance with her through the night to Augustana Hospital where the surgical emergency team, alerted by the police, awaited them.

He had lost a patient earlier on that same evening. It was a little girl who had fought for life against leukemia. She died quietly at home held securely in her father's arms while her mother read Janet's favorite story, *Good Night, Moon*, and said her bedtime prayers.

Simon had stayed with them, for they were friends, making the necessary telephone calls. Then he sat quietly in the living room of the small house while the grieving parents talked about Janet.

48

His mother would have said that there was a pattern in God's plan, but that we humans seldom recognized it. He had been on his way home, raging inwardly at the world's inadequacies, when he had come upon the accident and heard the faint call from the wrecked station wagon. There had been so small a margin of safety—four minutes at the very most—before the vehicle had exploded in flames.

Two people owed their lives to this girl and, Simon pondered, he had been able to save hers. Young Janet had died but Jenna lived. Sometime he might tell her the whole story of that night.

The days passed. Gradually all the bits and pieces of equipment which had helped her live left the room. The local-anesthetic injections to block the nerves near her fractured ribs were stretched out now to one in twenty-four hours, then only intermittently for pain.

And there *was* pain—when she coughed and when she practiced the breathing exercises. But the ribs had begun to knit.

Dr. Randall came in to explain to her that normal pulmonary function had been restored, but they must keep checking to be certain that full expansion of the lung was maintained. The likelihood of the leak reopening lessened now with each day that passed, he assured her. She had been fortunate, too, in that no infection had developed.

"I think he said that I'm breathing normally again," Jenna commented to Simon, who had stopped in to see her and found her in her robe and sitting in the armchair near the window.

She looked wistfully out at the May morning. "It's spring."

He nodded. "Even in northern Wisconsin."

Everything about Simon interested her. "You've been there recently?" she asked him, watching the dark brown eyes light up.

That was where he had been the weekend before, he explained. He told her about growing up in rural Wisconsin in the northern resort-lake area where his father had practiced medicine, of going east to Harvard for college, and then on to the medical school of the University of Wisconsin, of a small, well-loved cottage he still owned on a northern Wisconsin lake named Little Bay near a tiny place called Echo Station, about ten miles from the town of Minowac.

"Population 800," Simon said.

Jenna wondered, "How can you bear to live in the big city with such a place to go to? It must have wildflowers and tall fir trees and deer that come at twilight." She sounded wistful.

"A little matter of earning a living perhaps?" he suggested wryly.

He wanted to know how she was feeling and she told him. She also told him how hard it was for Blake and Daphne to manage without her. She needed to get home. He listened thoughtfully, asked more questions, and learned a great deal more about the Wilsons than Jenna ever realized.

She found herself describing their former home and her pleasure in the garden there. She told him about the Hamiltons, and her job, and how much better things were going to be now that Blake was getting established and Daphne's agency was calling her more steadily.

Like a wound-up toy unable to stop, she told him, too, about the dress at Greensleeves and the trip to the hairdresser.

"Ah, yes," Simon murmured. "The forty-dollar hair."

She turned to him, astonished. "However—?" she began.

He stood up then and bent his head to look directly at her.

She said, "I'll be going home soon, I think."

Simon stared at her, frowning.

"Is something wrong?" she asked, faintly.

He shook his head and was on his way. "Good-bye, hyacinth-girl."

She watched for him, hoping he would be back in the afternoon, but he did not come. Miss Sanchez, popping into her pretty mouth a Godiva chocolate from the box Martha Hamilton had thoughtfully provided, told Jenna that she had seen Dr. Fraser at lunch with Dr. Randall. They were having a serious discussion.

"Dr. Fraser is your very good friend, yes?" giggled Miss Sanchez.

Jenna did not answer. She was wondering if she would ever see Simon again after she left the hospital.

Dr. Randall came in the morning, and the head nurse was beside him. After a thorough examination he announced he was very satisfied with her progress and that she could be discharged anytime the next day. He closed his bag with a snap and addressed the nurse. "I think we'll have the senator in now, Miss Howland."

Jenna's eyes widened in surprise.

Parker Hamilton came close to the bed, leaned over and kissed her cheek. "That's from Martha." He smiled at her and placed a gift-wrapped box of chocolates in her lap. "And that's from me."

Dr. Randall lost no time in fancy explanations. She could leave the hospital tomorrow, he told her, but he warned that there was still a rather long convalescence ahead of her.

51

"How long?" Jenna felt apprehension.

With her history of pneumonia as a child and again just the previous year, the thoracic surgeon thought that she should plan on another two, perhaps even three, months. Probably two more months of rest and quiet, fresh air, and gradually increasing activities.

Jenna clenched her hands. "But I can't. That is, my job—"

"And that's why I'm here," Mr. Hamilton hastened to say. He went on to explain very calmly about sick leave and her paycheck continuing and comforting things like that. He told her that she owed it to herself to get well, fully well, and that her job would be waiting for her just as soon as Dr. Randall assured them that she could safely return to work.

"Paid sick leave for two months?" Jenna was astounded.

"Well, yes," the old gentleman replied. "This is your sixth year with us, you know, Jennifer Anne. And there will be the insurance money, too."

He had taken the liberty of putting wheels in motion, he explained to them, and would be representing Miss Wilson from now on in all legal and insurance matters pertaining to the accident.

Jenna, her eyes full of tears, thanked him. "I don't want to make money out of this accident," she reminded him. "Just, perhaps, if I could replace my car? And then, if that's proper, have some help with all these huge medical bills?" She looked apologetically at Dr. Randall.

Mr. Hamilton assured her that in his hands it would all be done most properly, and she sighed with relief because she knew that that was true.

"Now then," the attorney continued, "it appears that Mr. Redford of our office is taking his wife to Europe this summer for three months. And Mrs. Babcock, his private secretary, has suggested that in his absence she will be quite able to take care of my needs. Moreover, if there is an overload, a Miss—er—Elsa Hamperdinch instructs me to let you know that she'll give Mrs. Babcock immediate assistance."

"How very kind. Please tell them so for me. And you and Martha—always so kind—" Jenna's voice was trembling now.

The men's eyes met above her head and the surgeon nodded. The two of them shook hands, and Mr. Hamilton said good-bye and that she was not to worry about anything at all, that he'd be in close touch with her all the time.

Dr. Randall stayed on a few minutes. "The rib-belt will give you enough support for comfort, but not too tight, mind." He reminded her to continue her breathing exercises and warned her to be sure to get ample rest, and then gave her a little appointment card to come in as an out-patient for X rays and a checkup in one week.

Jenna telephoned Blake at work and told him the good news about the discharge. He reminded her that he had no car to come and get her, and that she had better plan to call a taxi.

She wished that he had thought to say he would come up to help. When she hesitantly suggested it, Blake agreed immediately.

After that, Jenna walked up and down the hospital corridor twice. Then she shed her robe and lay down on her bed, thinking. She'd have to call Daphne later to send up some clothes. It didn't seem quite proper, somehow, to get into a taxi in bathrobe and slippers.

She lay quietly, watching people pass in the corridor and worrying a little about why she could not return to work in another week. By the time a crisp knock sounded on her half-open door, she had fretted herself into a headache.

"Come in," she called.

Into the room came a slender, attractive woman in a softly tailored, lightweight apricot wool suit with a magnificent old-fashioned brooch of sapphires and diamonds gleaming on one lapel. A chic little hat of apricot wool was atop her beautifully styled dark hair.

"Dear child, what have you done to yourself?" There was genuine concern in the husky voice.

Jenna swallowed. It couldn't be! She turned quite pink and her lovely green eyes opened very wide. "Madame? Is it you, Madame Green?"

"It is I." The woman leaned forward and touched Jenna's hair. "So becoming. I am glad." She frowned. "You did not return, so I must come to you."

Jenna motioned that she should be seated. "But how did you know? I mean, who told you that I was here?"

Her visitor considered for a moment and then laughed softly. "I do not read minds, but I can—how do you say? Put together two and two.

"A tall man comes in the salon and demands a pink dress—a pink dress that was in our window almost six weeks ago! He is a mad man. Clarice calls me so that I may tell him so. He does not even know the size for this pink dress he must have, only that it is to be the very one that was in the window on a rainy April day when some girl saw it and wanted it." The dark eyes sparkled. " 'It is to go with her forty-dollar hair,' he says.

"The dress is not for sale, I tell him. I am saving it as a present for a young lady—under certain conditions." The sharp eyes considered the girl. "It will not fit you yet, but it is time for you to have the dress, Jenna Wilson. It is my gift to the girl with much courage."

Her cool lips brushed Jenna's flushed cheek. "You are to get well. That first. *Then* come to see me in the pink dress."

"Oh, I promise. Thank you—thank you so very much."

Madame lifted one dark eyebrow. "That young man will be worth the effort," she announced firmly and departed. On Jenna's coverlet she left a long rectangular box, beautifully tied with a huge moss-green satin bow.

Chapter 4

Simon was waiting for her shortly after ten o'clock when Jenna finished her shower. "All packed? Let's go," he said.

"Blake's coming for me," she told him, trying to keep the disappointment out of her voice. She placed the hairbrush and comb in her small case. "I'm so sorry, Simon. You've come all this way for nothing."

"I called Daphne last night to tell Blake I'd save him the trip."

"Oh," she said, wondering a little what they had talked about.

"Something the matter?"

"No—well, not really. But I'll have to go home in my robe and slippers. You see, Daphne was to send my clothes with Blake." She asked doubtfully, "Will that be all right?"

"No problem," he declared comfortably. His eyes swept the room. "Got all your things? Do these flowers come along?"

The vase of pink roses was to go to the old man in the next room, she said, and asked him to wait a moment while she went there to tell him good-bye. When she returned, Miss Sanchez had arrived with a wheelchair and Jenna rode off in style, leaving Mrs. Hamilton's latest box of Godiva chocolates at the nurses' station for them to enjoy.

A pale yellow Porsche 911 was pulled up to the curb at the circle entrance to the hospital. Miss Sanchez exclaimed ecstatically at its sleek lines and handsome finish.

Simon opened the curbside door and stowed Jenna's case. A large yellow Labrador lifted his head. He was a beautiful dog, his bright coat smooth and shining. "Good boy," Simon patted him. "Hop back. You're in Jenna's seat."

"He's yours?" Jenna was enchanted. "I love yellow Labs." She wanted to stroke his coat and let him smell her hand, but the Porsche was pulling away from the curb and she looked out the side window, waving good-bye to Miss Sanchez.

Simon's glance flickered toward her. "Warm enough? You can put up the window."

"No, I'm fine. I like fresh air." She put her head back and sighed with pure pleasure. "It's so wonderful to be going home. And what a heavenly car. Have you had it long?"

They were in noontime traffic, threading their way through the crowded streets, and Simon answered her, keeping his eyes straight ahead. It was something about the Porsche being a wise choice, for it made the trip north in record time, safely and comfortably as well.

"North" must mean up to the cottage on Little Bay Lake, Jenna thought, watching with pleasure the way Simon drove, effortlessly and with great skill. It sounded as if he went north rather frequently.

Well, and who wouldn't? she asked herself silently,

56

staring at the dingy red-brick buildings of the section of the great city through which they were traveling. Late May in northern Wisconsin—there'd be violets in the woods and new green growth leafing out on trees and shrubs now.

"West on Augusta, right?" he asked abruptly.

They would be home in another fifteen minutes. She smiled warmly at him and told him how much she appreciated his generous help. "I'm afraid you've missed all sorts of appointments," she said quietly in her lovely voice.

"All arranged," he corrected her smoothly.

She didn't know exactly what he meant by that, and it hardly seemed the right time to ask him about his work, so she put her hand out and patted the Lab who sat very still, his head resting against Simon's right shoulder. "Left here," she directed him. "One block, then take a right. We're the middle apartment house—there, up ahead."

She dug in her purse for her keys and Simon took them from her and reached in for her case.

"The dog—may he come in?" she asked.

"He'll stay in the car."

Jenna was disappointed. That probably meant that Simon was in a hurry to get away. They were friends, but she must not presume on this wonderful, new friendship. She said carefully, "Yes, of course. Has he a name?" She thought he answered to "goldfish," but she must have been mistaken.

Simon took her arm as they climbed the steps to her door. "I suggest you go straight to bed," he said in a very professional-sounding voice. "Don't make the mistake of doing too much this first day you're home. Daphne will be in around five, she says. She'll get your dinner."

When he unlocked the door, Jenna put out a hand

57

to steady herself, and Simon saw it and frowned. "Bed," he ordered crisply.

The little living room had a neglected air. No one had bothered to vacuum and Daphne had forgotten to water the spectacular fuchsia plant, which drooped down with a decidedly dead look. A huge pile of unfolded laundry was on the dining table near the window and an untidy stack of opened mail waited on her desk.

Simon saw her glance rest on the envelopes. "Later," he said and took her by the arm again. "Bed. Which way?"

The small bedroom would always seem crowded with their two beds and two dressers, a bedside table, and their mother's antique blanket chest, but this was really too bad, Jenna thought weakly. Daphne's bed was still unmade and her own bed overflowed with dress cartons, shoe boxes, lingerie, and bright plastic containers of pantyhose.

Simon's lips tightened. "We'll make short work of this," he muttered, sweeping boxes and cartons to the floor. He pulled back the spread and blanket, smoothed out the sheet, and said, "In you go."

With a deep sigh Jenna slipped out of her robe and into bed. It felt wonderful. She closed her eyes. From the kitchen she heard cupboard doors banging, the crash of a metal pan, water running. When she opened her eyes, Simon stood by her bed with a cup of hot tea.

"I must go—appointments, errands," he said vaguely, anxious now to be gone.

She thrust out her hands, clinging to his, hating good-byes and wishing that she would see him again—but without much hope. The expression on his face was impossible to read.

She heard the door close and then she slept. An hour later she awakened, hungry. She sat up in bed, ignor-

58

ing the appalling mess on the floor, and debated what she would like for her lunch. Maybe a soft-cooked egg. Or cinnamon toast? Thinking of cinnamon toast made her mouth water. Jenna decided there was nothing she would like better.

The refrigerator held a half-quart of milk, one English muffin, some strawberry jelly, and an old fragment of Cheshire cheese. Jenna searched the cupboards. Not even a loaf of bread! The refrigerator's freezer section, where she always kept the makings of at least one emergency meal, was completely empty.

She made herself a cup of tea, added milk, and sat down to drink it at the kitchen table while the solitary English muffin toasted. Blake, when he came home, was going to have to go for groceries; he could call a taxi. It cost the earth to eat out. What *had* they been thinking of?

Simon had found the sink full of dirty breakfast dishes. A week of breakfast dishes, she realized with chagrin. They dripped dry now on the drainboard. He had neatly rinsed out the scrubber and the dishcloth, and hung a dish towel to dry.

While eating the muffin, Jenna wished she were back at Augustana, looking forward to an attractive dinner tray and a long nap. Then, on her way back to bed she started to pick up the mail, intending to sort out the bills, but changed her mind. "Maybe tomorrow," she said aloud. She had no energy left today.

The sound of a key being fitted into the lock, and Daphne's laughter, awakened her. Hearing the deeper tones of a man's voice, she slipped into an old blue robe.

It was early for Blake. The little bedside clock read "five." Jenna brushed her hair, tied the blue flannel belt around her waist, and wandered into the kitchen.

"Darling Jenna, you're home!" Daphne deposited a huge bag of groceries on the kitchen table and rushed to embrace her, carefully, so the ribs would not protest.

Jenna stood still, watching Daphne and Simon carry in more brown bags that appeared to be filled with oranges, bacon, bread, milk, apples, eggs, detergent, Kleenex, canned soup, packages of meat for the freezer, frozen waffles, butter—

"Butter . . . why not margarine?" Jenna asked.

"Butter?" Daphne was momentarily surprised, but she recovered quickly. "Oh, I guess we're celebrating your being home. Wasn't it lucky I met Simon? All these groceries! I could never have managed on my own without a car."

"Do you live near our supermarket?" Jenna asked him with just a trace of suspicion in her mind.

"Not too far." He smiled.

That could mean anything. She supposed that with a Porsche distance was all relative anyway.

Daphne was unpacking canned goods and inspecting labels with interest. "Wait till you see the delicious dinner I'm going to make you. How's shrimp bisque for a starter? And Simon's brought a bottle of wine."

He placed a hand on Jenna's shoulder, turning her to face him. "You're tired . . . did you nap?" He led her gently back to bed. "Let Daphne cope, she's quite able."

Blake arrived just before dinner. He brought Jenna's meal in on a large tray, propping up pillows behind her. "Good to see you home again. Maybe now we can get organized around here."

"I haven't looked at the mail yet. Many bills?"

He said, "Now why do you want to worry about bills on your first day home?"

"There seemed such a lot—"

60

"Tomorrow's time enough to talk about it." His eyes avoided hers. "Daphne's got our dinner ready. See you later."

But later there was the continued hum of the vacuum cleaner. Jenna got up and brushed her teeth, loosened the Velcro fasteners of the rib-belt a little, changed into a fresh nightgown, and quickly sank down into the blessed darkness of sleep.

She did not waken when Simon came in to say goodbye, standing quietly looking down at her in the dim light from the dresser lamp.

Later, there was noise. In her dreams Blake called out angrily, ". . . Trying to run our lives for us." And a voice like Daphne's, but tight with fury, shrilled an answer. Jenna stirred but did not awaken.

She found the bill for the new car two days later. It had been tucked into the compartment of the desk where she kept stationery, and a corner of the envelope caught her eye. Seven thousand dollars! The bill was made out to her; payment was pending.

She confronted Blake that night. "We can't afford an Oldsmobile Cutlass, not even a used one."

"For God's sake, we're not paupers. This is a good deal, the car's a demo. A new model, deluxe. And we *need* to have a car."

"You had no right—" She sat back in the armchair and tried again. "There's no money yet to replace my car. It has to go back, Blake. Take it back tomorrow."

"You'll be getting the insurance money any day now."

"Blake, it will be months before it's all straightened out. You told me that yourself. And Mr. Hamilton knows that I want the first money to go toward all my medical bills."

"That old man, he's—" Before he could protest further, Daphne rushed in. She let out a wail when she saw her sister.

"Shut up, for heaven's sake!" Blake yelled at her. "What's the matter?"

Daphne sank down on the floor and hid her face in Jenna's lap. Her shoulders shook with uncontrolled weeping.

Jenna tried to calm her. She stroked the shining blonde head and murmured consolingly, "You'll make yourself ill if you cry so. What's happened, Daphne? Tell us—we can't help you if we don't know."

The words spilled out between the sobs. "It's Don . . . all over. . . . He says he can't afford to marry yet . . . and then . . . and then . . ."

She lifted her head and her pretty face was blotched and streaked with tears. "He can't do this. I won't let him do this to me!" She began to cry again.

"Women!" Blake threw up his hands and left the apartment. Somehow Jenna got Daphne off to bed.

There was little sleep for Jenna that night. She tossed and turned, wincing at the pain. Echoes of the day haunted her. *Seven thousand for a car!* If Blake would not, she must return it to the dealer herself. To-morrow—or the next day. She dreaded the idea of driving again.

And this business of Daphne and Don. It had progressed so quickly, and now it seemed that Don was having second thoughts. Daphne was upset, naturally. How much of what Daphne had said did she really mean, Jenna wondered.

I want to go away. Get out of this miserable town for a while—England or California—Let me go to California, Jenna—You have the money—Blake says you'll have enough for lots of things we need—

You have the money . . . you have the money . . . money . . . money . . .

Jenna got up and paced the living-room floor. It was nearly dawn. She drifted sadly out to the kitchen and made herself hot tea.

Blake found her sitting at the kitchen table writing checks when he came out at seven. "Sorry about last night," he said. "Did she ever settle down? Did you get some rest?"

"Not much."

"They'll patch it up." He fixed his breakfast in silence and ate it rapidly, looking at her across the table.

"Can I get you anything before I leave for the office?" He stood there, nervously swinging the car keys.

"No thanks, Blake. Blake, about the car—"

He swung around angrily and made for the door. "Later. Okay?"

Daphne came out of the bedroom around ten o'clock, dressed for a modeling assignment. "Blake gone?" She peeled an orange carefully, watchful of the juice.

Jenna nodded.

"Damn . . . I wanted a ride." She yawned delicately. "I can't sleep with you getting up all the time during the night. Up and down. Up and down. I need my rest."

Jenna wrote out the June rent check, sealed the last of the envelopes, and attached the stamps. "Sorry."

Daphne tapped a manicured finger on the kitchen table, thinking. "That Greensleeves box in our closet, what's in it?"

"A dress I intend to wear in about two months."

Her sister's face twisted with anger. "Simon? Do you mean you're thinking of marrying Simon in two months? Is that what you mean? That old busybody! Coming over here and ordering us around, telling Blake and me how to run our lives."

Jenna looked astonished. "Marry Simon? Simon's a friend. And what do you mean, trying to run our lives. He's not been here since the day I came home from the hospital. Has he?" She closed her eyes for a moment. "I've meant to ask you, Daphne. Those groceries that night—"

Daphne bit her lip. "Forget it, will you?" She gave Jenna a quick good-bye kiss. "I've got to dash. Try to catch a nap, why don't you? You look ghastly."

At the door she turned back for a moment. "I meant what I said last night. It's either England or California—*you* decide. California might be cheaper. If you can afford frocks from Greensleeves, you don't need to worry about money, I guess."

Jenna paid the cab driver, adding a modest tip, and stepped out on the parkway in front of Augustana. It was warm to be only June second. The morning sun felt good on her arms.

She found her way to Outpatients and reported in. Half an hour later, with the laboratory tests done and the X rays completed, a helpful Candystriper directed her to Dr. Randall's hospital office.

Jenna's eyes searched the corridors, hoping she might cross paths with Simon. It had been seven whole days since he had come to dinner, seven days that she had been home.

Dr. Randall greeted her, then bent over to study her folder. He rang for a nurse and Jenna went off with her to the tiny cubicle where she donned the hospital gown.

The surgeon spoke little during the examination. He referred frequently to the six X rays suspended on a lighted frame.

"Appetite back?" he queried. "Cough . . . again. Once again. Hurt here? Here?" His hands were gentle.

64

"How's the rib-belt? Giving you enough support?" He positioned the stethoscope in various spots and listened. "Let's see you do your breathing exercise next." He watched her face the wall, creep her fingers up, centimeter by centimeter. "That far, eh? Not too bad."

After she had dressed she came to sit by his desk. She watched him make notes in her folder, get up and study the X rays once more, return to his desk and write again.

At length he closed the folder, put his elbows up on the desk, and rested his chin in his folded hands.

"Well?" Jenna asked nervously.

"The ribs are coming along fine," he explained. He added that the lung was maintaining expansion, which was an excellent sign. Her weight was down a little, but that was all right as long as she was eating properly so that bones would knit and tissue would heal.

Jenna nodded.

"Now the not-so-good news," said Dr. Randall, watching her closely. He told her that her color was poor, her pulse was fast, and her blood pressure was higher than he liked.

He said, "Either you're being too active too soon, or you're not resting enough, or you're worrying too much. Or all three.

"It will delay your full recovery," the surgeon warned. "Go back to bed as soon as you return home, take a long nap, and make a concerted effort to do less and rest more. It's up to you how quickly you will recover."

He rose and shook hands with her. "I'll want to see you in about two weeks," he said.

All the way home Jenna forced herself to remain calm. Determined not to cry in public she paid the taxi and hastily ran up the steps to the apartment. She felt dreadfully let down. And worried. Dr. Randall could not have been more explicit: If she expected to get well, something had to change.

Perhaps she could move her bed out to the small screened porch off the kitchen. The idea of a night's sleep uninterrupted by Daphne's comings and goings was a blissful one. Jenna measured the space with her eyes. The bed would fit. But when it rained? And how about the neon lights from the corner bar?

Well, drug stores sold eye-masks—she'd seen them. And perhaps Blake could fashion plastic sheets to keep out the rain.

She felt torn with uncertainty. If only she were not so tired . . .

First she'd tidy up the apartment a little. She got out soap, cleanser, and a pail of warm water, found the long-handled sponge mop and began to clean the kitchen and the bathroom floors. Next she thought about lunch and decided she was not hungry after all. Maybe after a rest—

A knocking on the door penetrated her dreams at last and she sat up in bed, surprised to see that she was still in the yellow knit dress in which she had gone to the hospital. Fuzzy with sleep, she called, "Who is it?" through the door.

"Simon."

His discerning eyes searched her face, and he shook his head. "Sleeping? You look as if you need another forty hours—straight."

"Oh, you brought the dog." Jenna knelt down and smoothed his yellow coat. "What's his name?"

"Goldfisch. What did Dr. Randall say this morning?"

She said uncertainly, "I keep thinking you say 'goldfish.' Simon, it's so good to see you again. I thought you'd decided to forget all about me." She amended that hastily. " . . . About us."

66

He came into the kitchen and studied the clean, wet floor. "You're either a glutton for punishment or you want to die young." He was pale with a controlled anger.

She said quietly, in a very practical tone of voice, "Gradually increasing activities, right? Well, who's to say if those activities are a walk in the park or a little bit of housework?"

He looked at her as if she were a very dull child. "So how did Randall find you?"

"The ribs are knitting satisfactorily and the lung expansion is being maintained, Dr. Randall said, and that pleased him . . ." Her voice trailed off a bit.

"What an uncommonly bad memory you have."

"You didn't give me a chance to finish!" Tears welled up in her eyes.

"What else?"

She hesitated. "Oh, you know, Simon—all the usual things, like be sure to get enough sleep and eat the proper foods, and—and don't worry."

He demanded, "And you're prepared to follow his instructions?"

She said shakily, "Oh, Simon, what *am* I going to do?"

He placed a hand under her chin and lifted up her unhappy face, gently wiping away some of the tears that were sliding down her cheeks. "It's too much for you. I've been afraid of that."

"I thought I was doing so well." Her voice was anguished. "But it's true—I'm not sleeping much lately. I mean to, and I'm weary enough to, but the minute the light goes out I—I—and Blake's angry with me because I won't keep the car." She sniffed and sobbed, "Did you know about the car?"

"Tell me," he suggested gently.

So it all came out, and Simon listened until she was

67

finished, observing the high color that now stained her cheeks.

As she talked, the Lab came close and placed his head in her lap. Jenna looked down at him, and tears began anew.

Simon said quietly, "You're upsetting Goldfisch."

Jenna gasped and shook her head as if to clear it. "You *did* say goldfish!"

He laughed at her. "Goldfisch. With a 'c' in it. It's your name, isn't it, boy?"

The tail thumped firmly in a kind of affirmative.

He had been looking for a larger apartment a year or so ago, he explained, and had found one he liked in a remodeled town house out in Oak Park. "The owner herself lived in one of the apartments," Simon said, "and she liked the idea of a 'doctor in the house,' as she put it. 'I don't allow pets, of course,' she told me, and I admitted right away that I had Goldfisch. She just laughed and said that naturally she would not object to that. I took her at her word and signed the lease, and when we started moving in, she came raging, sputtering mad, and I immediately introduced her to Goldfisch. She was livid. 'You know I thought you meant goldfish,' she said."

"Oh, that was wicked of you," Jenna giggled. "Then what?"

"Well, I showed her his papers, and finally she said we could stay and that he would be the official guard dog. So we moved in."

"We?"

"The dog and I," Simon said, watching her enjoyment of his story. He found himself wondering how he'd gotten so involved with this girl. He'd be telling her next about Patrice, he thought wryly.

"Papers? You mean he really *is* Goldfisch?"

"With a 'c.' His sire is Golden Lad of the famous

68

Fisch Isle Kennels in Canada and his dam is a Wyoming winner named Summer Gold. Look here." He reached in his pocket for something to write on, found an envelope, and sketched out the dog's bloodlines, explaining as he wrote that FC meant Field Champion, AFC stood for Amateur Field Champion, and the Ch indicated Bench Champion.

She was delighted. "He's a champion then, just like his parents?"

Simon's long fingers reached behind the dog's ears, caressing him roughly. "Well, no. When he was just a pup, he somehow tangled with an overlarge Doberman and got chewed up pretty badly. He's been splinted and patched; that's why I took him about three years ago. He's champion in spirit all the way through, but no, I'll never show him."

"Goldfisch!" The laughter started in her eyes and then bubbled joyously out of her throat. Simon grinned broadly.

She winced and caught her side. "Ooh, that hurt but it feels good too. I haven't laughed like that for so long." She wiped her eyes and said to them both, "You two are good for me. I'm feeling better already."

"Then it's a good time to tell you this," Simon remarked. "I had lunch with your surgeon. Randall thinks you need to get away, out of this apartment for a while. Out from under, Jenna."

He had caught her unawares, he could see. And that was good.

Startled, she echoed, "Away?"

"Somewhere out of the city where you'd have plenty of fresh air, a chance for more rest, less—er— responsibilities so close at hand."

Jenna gave a funny little laugh. "So you knew all along what Dr. Randall said." She turned her head away, choosing not to look at him as she answered,

"You must know it's impossible, Simon. Quite out of the question."

He touched her scarred cheek with his large, tanned hand and forced her to turn back to him. "You'll be no good to either Blake or Daphne if you don't get well. Nor to yourself, my dear. I have a plan, one that your boss thinks is a good idea too, but it has strings on it."

Jenna was fighting tears again. One more sign that she was overburdened, he thought angrily, and continued, "I want you to go up to my northern Wisconsin cottage on Little Bay Lake for a couple of months. It's lovely up there now, and it will get even more so as spring advances. You will be able to read and sleep and walk in the woods. Mostly, you can just rest and set your own pace with no one else to fret about. It's not much, just a cottage, but it's a year-round one and you'll be comfortable there. You can order groceries in from Echo Station by telephone, and I have friends nearby who'd see that you got anything you needed."

He paused a moment, trying to gauge her reaction. "Later you might enjoy some swimming in a little cove I'll show you. The town of Minowac is just thirteen or fourteen miles away. There's a physician I know there who can do the X rays and keep Randall posted on your progress."

She asked in a tight little voice, "And the strings on this offer?"

"Neither Blake nor Daphne is to know where you are."

It was not what she had expected. She thought carefully. "It creates so many problems—"

He interrupted her. "Not unless you let it do so. Mr. Hamilton plans to recommend that Blake return the Cutlass, then he'll arrange for the purchase of an inexpensive car for you. He'll tend to all that. You can write the July and August rent checks right now and leave them on your desk, along with a note to your brother and sister explaining that you have gone away to recuperate—and why. They will be kept informed of your progress by way of your letters to Martha Hamilton, who, incidentally, says to tell you that this plan has her blessing. Your sick-leave checks will be paid directly into your personal checking account and will more than cover the small expenses you'll have at the cottage."

He said smoothly, "Daphne and Blake are both working, and of course, can take care of expenses here, other than the rent." He reached out and caught her hand. "How soon can you be packed?"

"But have you thought—" she began. "Won't it be awkward for you?"

"You mean, what will people say?" he asked sharply, without allowing her to finish. "The people who count—the Hamiltons, Randall, you, and I—know that we are friends. *Friends*, Jenna."

"There's no one—no one who might misunderstand?" she asked a little stiffly.

He shook his head. She saw a kind of bleakness in his eyes.

"It would be heavenly," she murmured wistfully, thinking of blue skies and tall green fir trees and the wonderful scent of country in early June.

"Well, then?"

"You're sure it would be all right? For you, I mean? And how would I get there? I find I'm afraid to drive," she confessed.

He said reassuringly, "That's just a nervous reaction that will vanish when you feel completely well again. It's Friday; Goldfisch and I are taking you up. Now. Get packed. Be sure to have warm slacks and sweaters. Country clothes. A swimsuit for later. Anything you

71

forget you can buy up there. And the Hamiltons and I will handle things at this end."

"There's the laundry to sort," she said, worried again, "and I haven't done the breakfast dishes yet."

He steered her straight to the bedroom. "Two suitcases, no more," he ordered. "And we're leaving in thirty minutes."

Chapter 5

The drive to the lake country did not begin in thirty minutes. It was not until shortly before five when Simon turned the key in the lock and hurried Jenna to the car.

"Not too bad—for a woman," he declared, looking at his watch. "It's a trip of about 350 miles, some six hours or so of driving time. I recommend we stop for dinner en route, then drive straight through. All right with you?"

Everything and nothing was all right with Jenna, who at this moment felt all torn apart.

She had packed in the greatest rush, remembering heavy sweaters, then sat down at her desk to write the rent checks, the payment for the May telephone bill, and the letter to her sister and brother. The letter was very difficult to write, with both Simon and the dog pacing up and down, but finally Jenna tucked in a twenty-dollar bill and sealed the envelope. Uncertainty flooded over her, yet along with it came the knowledge that Simon had probably thought of everything.

She closed the apartment door once and then went running back, reappearing in a minute with a dress box and a small fuchsia plant in her arms. Simon stowed away the box in the front luggage compartment beside her two cases and his own duffelbag. The potted plant he placed in a clear plastic bag and tucked it in between the bucket seats.

The Lab leaped to the little space behind the seats, and Jenna scrambled in. Simon checked their seat belts, and the Porsche pulled smoothly away from the curbing.

"All right if we drive straight through?" Simon asked again.

Jenna considered the awkwardness of hotel bills and motel rooms and agreed at once. She relaxed and watched Simon's skillful driving and tried to blot out thoughts of Daphne arriving home to find the breakfast dishes still undone and no dinner started, and of what Blake would say when he read the letter.

Simon was wearing a brown-plaid driving cap to shade his eyes. He said, "Why not lie back and take a nap?"

"I don't want to miss my first glimpse of the country," Jenna protested.

It would be some time yet before they were on the Interstate, he reminded her, so she slid down a little in the leather seat and closed her eyes. She felt a warm muzzle touch her cheek, and she fell asleep knowing she was with friends.

The last rays of the sun were lengthening the shadows of fence posts and storage silos when she awakened. She looked out at great stretches of green grass and a herd of dairy cows moving homeward in single file. The Porsche flashed past orchards of apple trees and farms whose land ran even with Interstate 94.

A sign on their right pointed west off the superhighway to the towns of Union Grove, Kansasville, and Burlington.

"We're in Racine County now." Simon knew the

73

route by heart. "We're going to stop in Milwaukee for dinner. Feel like some great German cooking?"

He looked sideways at her. "Cat got your tongue?"

Her mouth felt dry as dust. Panic welled up inside her. Blake would be home by now. Jenna visualized the dreadful scene that was probably taking place in the apartment that very moment.

"Simon, I don't know what I was thinking of," she blurted out. "I must go back."

He uttered an oath under his breath. She heard part of it and cringed. "I'm sorry, but I must."

"I hear you." His face looked grim. "There's a lake about fifteen miles off to our left. I used to visit my uncle there when I was a boy. He was a physician in Chicago, kept a summer home there at Eagle Lake in a private colony of homes built around a golf course. That's where I learned to play golf. He never had the time. He was my father's older brother. Never liked large cities, but he had this big practice and made a lot of money."

She sat very still, wondering why he was telling her this.

"Full of plans, Uncle Josh—always was going to remodel that summer place, live there year 'round, grow roses, travel some with my aunt . . . "

The sun was setting. Coppery-pink clouds with streaks of palest gold massed on the horizon ahead. Miles slipped by. Jenna turned a little in the seat toward Simon. "And did he?"

Simon went on. "He took me into practice with him six years ago after my residency was completed. He was always determined that I wasn't going back up north, although my father was still alive then, and there was an opening in his office waiting for me. That's no place for a Harvard man, he'd argue with

74

my father, and my dad would just grin at him and say he personally knew one that it suited very well indeed.

"My father died three years ago. Mother soon after, as if she was too lonely without him. Uncle Josh swore then that he was remodeling their cottage that very next spring, that he intended to turn the entire practice over to me and retire early. You never saw a more surprised man than he was when he landed up in Augustana with a coronary. My aunt was in the room with him by the time I got there, and he was going fast. The last words he said, I guess, were to me. 'Timing . . . it's all a matter of timing, and don't you forget it, laddie.' "

It seemed suddenly important that she know. "He never got to grow the roses?"

"No roses. It's all a matter of timing, Jenna, just as he warned."

"I still must go back."

They crossed into Milwaukee County, traveling fast, and the road veered slightly to the right, toward Lake Michigan again. Jenna watched the country scenes slip away to become the suburban outskirts of Milwaukee.

"We'll have dinner first, talk later," Simon was saying. "There are two restaurants here that are specially famous for German-style cooking—Karl Ratzche's and Maders. We're probably nearer Maders," he said, swinging the car into the exit lane of the Interstate and heading into the downtown area of the city itself.

Maders was crowded with Friday-night diners, but the host found them a pleasant table near the stairway and a waitress brought Simon a tall folder. Jenna read everything printed on the huge menu, then begged him to order for her.

By tacit agreement it was to be a traditionally German meal. Simon chose *leberknödel suppe*, red cabbage, and *sauerbraten* with caraway-seeded noodles, to be served with a lightly chilled, full-bodied white burgundy.

Over their platters of green salad garnished with a sampling of thin slices of sausage, Simon explained that *leberknödel suppe* was liver-ball soup. *Sauerbraten* she knew, of course, to be the marinated spiced beef roast with gingersnap-thickened gravy.

"Mmm, can't decide," Jenna murmured later when their waitress brought the dessert cards. Simon suggested *Salzburger nockerl* because girls, he said, always liked its fluffy richness sprinkled all over with powdered vanilla sugar. He was going to have Liederkranz cheese and crackers.

Jenna finally decided on a tiny portion of *apfel kuchen* with a cinnamon ice cream sauce.

When they were having coffee, she admitted, "I was really hungry and everything tasted simply splendid. Thank you, Simon."

He signaled the waitress. "Now that we've eaten, do we need to talk? I'm not going to argue, Jenna, nor do I go in for kidnapping. You know exactly why you need to go away, but the decision is yours."

She felt sudden anger and a new despair. Her white face turned up to him. "North," she whispered.

"Good girl."

Twilight deepened to dusk as the Porsche regained the Interstate and streaked westward. It was a beautiful night, with a half moon for company. A distinct freshness filled the air coming in through the open car windows, and Jenna sensed that they were moving farther and farther from the great industrial cities along Lake Michigan.

Eighty minutes later they circled the eastern suburbs of Madison and turned sharply north again. "Soon

76

we'll be halfway home." Simon's voice held a satisfied tone.

Near Portage they stopped for gas and cups of hot coffee before continuing north on US 51. Jenna exercised Goldfisch on his leash while Simon found water for the dog's bowl.

It felt good to stretch the cramps from their legs, but Simon was eager to be moving again. "I'd like to get home before two o'clock," he said. "Ready?"

From then on Jenna drowsed. Simon flicked off the car radio and drove in silence. Miles flew past.

"Where are we?" she asked him sleepily. Simon was singing logging folk songs, and his voice sounded loud in her ear.

" . . . On the banks of the Little Eau Pleine!" he sang in a deep baritone, laughing down at her. He said, "We're just past Stevens Point and heading into Wausau. This is old lumbering country. Won't be long now."

"How far?"

"Another seventy miles or so."

Outside of Wausau they found an all-night diner and stopped again so that Jenna could stretch her legs and do some deep breathing. Between sips of scalding coffee, Simon showed her on the map where they were. He ticked off the towns: "Merrill, Tomahawk, Hazelhurst, Minocqua, Minowac." Roughing Goldfisch's yellow coat, he promised, "Not much longer, old boy. Not much longer."

To Jenna he said, "You can't see them because it's night, but this road runs right through the lake country. Several hundred lakes, some of the most beautiful scenery in this nation."

An hour later he sang out, "Minowac! Wake up, Jenna, we're almost there."

He was as eager as a young boy going fishing for the

first time, she thought, sitting up and finger-combing her hair. She noticed raindrops on the windshield. The car was traveling much more slowly now: on a hard-topped road, then onto a gravel one, finally off onto a narrow dirt road.

Simon stopped the Porsche and looked at his watch. It was one forty-five. He opened the door and Gold-fisch twisted past him and raced off into the darkness, barking madly.

Simon laughed. "Checking up on his chipmunks." He left the headlights on to light their path, and Jenna stepped out onto pine needles and soft earth.

She could smell the pines and the scent of flowers. Lilacs? Could it possibly be lilac wafted on the rain-cold breeze?

In the beams of the Porsche's headlights she could see the rear of a white Cape Cod-style cottage, with a wing on one side and a dark slanting roofline. It stood in a clearing back from the little road in its own world of peace and quiet. The cottage was larger than she had imagined it would be. Somehow she had been thinking of a very small place, a sort of hideaway cabin of two or three rooms.

Simon had gone on ahead and, as she watched, lights came on in one room, then another. The windows glowed a welcome.

"Come on up," Simon called, "I'll get your cases in a minute."

Jenna went slowly up the two steps of the small back stoop. Simon was holding the door open for her. "Welcome," he said, and drew her in, the dog at her heels, through a pine-paneled kitchen and into the living room beyond. At one end, in the massive fireplace built of river stone, flames already flickered in the kindling beneath the birch logs. A large sofa and two comfortable wing chairs were placed invitingly before the fire.

"There won't be warm water for a shower yet—I've just now put the fuses in—and anyway I want you to get to bed without delay, so wash your face and brush your teeth like a good child while I heat water and make us some hot tea." He motioned with his free hand. "The bathroom's here off the living room, and you're to have this bedroom. It's the one toward the lake."

He disappeared then to get her luggage and Jenna pushed open the bedroom door he had indicated. The room was chilly, like the rest of the house, and she was glad to see extra woolen blankets piled at the foot of the beautiful four-poster spool bed.

It was rather a large room, and Jenna's first impression was of a room filled with an unusually fine assortment of furniture for a vacation cottage. But then Simon used the place year 'round. Perhaps that made a difference, she reminded herself as she admired a marble-topped table piled high with books and a splendid broken-pediment highboy, a chest-on-chest that was probably cherrywood.

She placed her handbag carefully down on a delicate walnut dressing table with satinwood cross-bandings, wondering as she did so who the beautiful girl was in the silver-framed photograph on the small bedside table.

When Simon came in with her luggage, she unpacked just enough to find her blue flannel robe, a brushed nylon nightgown, and warm slippers. Carrying her clothes and her toilet kit, she located the bathroom.

Simon was busy in the kitchen. Faintly, she heard a teakettle whistle and the rattle of china, then the slam of a screen door and the undertones of his voice as he talked to the Lab.

She came out into the living room. Simon was sitting on the raised stone hearth, his arm around the dog. A tray with two steaming mugs was by his side. "Good—you look warmer. There's brandy in yours," he warned, standing up. "To make you sleep."

She finished her tea, put down the mug, and said, "I think I'd sleep, brandy or no. The silence of this place . . . no cars roaring up and down the street, no neon lights. Utter peace."

"Yes." Simon reached into his jacket pocket. "Do you have a flashlight? Keep this one on the bedside table in case you get up in the night."

She yawned and he said, "Get to bed. Leave your door open. You'll have warmth from the fire that way. Goldfisch sleeps in, so don't worry if you hear him padding around."

He was leaning over, putting the fire guard into place. Jenna reached down and stroked the dog. "Simon—I—I want to say thank you."

He looked up, startled. There was an awkward silence. He said somewhat curtly, "You're exhausted." She felt a light kiss brush her cheek.

"Thank you, Simon. For everything."

"We'll talk about it tomorrow. Sleep well," he said.

She slipped into bed and the unexpected warmth of a hot-water bottle touched her toes. Leaning on one elbow, she reached out for the light switch of the bedside lamp and noticed then that the photograph of the gorgeous brunette was gone. Taken away . . .

Jenna lay still, thinking. A slice of moonlight shone through her partly opened window, and a bird called from the tall evergreens beyond the clearing.

She fell asleep with her face turned toward the open door, watching the reflected glow of the fire, breath-

80

ing the fragrance of burning birch logs and blissfully aware of being delightfully warm.

When Jenna awoke the next morning, with sunshine on the coverlet and the aroma of coffee in the air, the Baby Ben on the table said nine o'clock. Nine o'clock! She hadn't slept that late in weeks.

She got out of bed, feeling the chill in the morning air, and scuffed into the sheepskin slippers. Wrapping the robe about her, she crossed to the sliding glass door leading out onto some kind of wooden deck.

Beyond the deck was the shoreline of the lake—great rocky boulders with water lapping against them—and beyond that, the lake itself, bright with morning sunshine. On the far side of Little Bay she saw fir trees, masses of them standing against the blue of the sky.

It was a glorious sight and she drew in a deep breath, feeling wonderful. She made short work of a shower and dressed quickly in warm black slacks and a white wool pullover, heavy socks, and her Norwegian mocs.

On the side of the house a little path curved off into the woods beyond the clearing. Jenna brushed her hair by the dresser, looking out the window and wondering where the path led, and saw Simon in blue jeans and a thick blue pullover come out of the woods with the Lab at his heels.

She met him by the back door, holding it open and smiling at him, seeing the places where his sweater had begun to unravel.

"You're looking much better than yesterday morning," he commented, pleased. "Sleep well?"

"Very well." Yesterday morning was an age away already, she thought, crouching down to hug Goldfisch and asking, "What's for breakfast?"

81

He kept his voice expressionless, but she could see laughter in the dark eyes. "Hungry, eh? Settle for coffee for a starter?" He pointed to the electric coffee pot on the kitchen cupboard, its warming light glowing red. "You can pour me a second, if you will. Two sugars, no cream."

She offered, "If you'd tell me what to fix for breakfast, I'd be glad to do the cooking." She thought hopefully of hickory-smoked bacon, country sausage, golden scrambled eggs—

Simon said, "Breakfast is in town this morning. I've made a shopping list."

Of course! How silly can you get, she rebuked herself. He'd only connected the electricity when they arrived. Naturally the refrigerator was bare. She went to collect her purse. "Does Goldfisch come?"

The Lab was to stay in the cottage this trip, Simon said, and checked the dog's water bowl. "Ready?"

She thought perhaps he had forgotten. "Don't we lock up?" She was practically running to keep up with his long strides.

Simon started the Porsche, turned the wheel, and they shot out of the clearing into the little road. "The dog's there," he told her. "We don't go much for locking up around here, except when we leave, of course. I don't think I've ever heard of any problems out this way."

He was frowning. "When you're there alone, however, I expect you to observe all sensible precautions. Lock the doors when you leave the house, even for just a stroll, and lock up at night. Those are orders."

"Yes," she promised, watching how the tall pines marched close to their narrow road, catching a glimpse of blue sky above only if she looked straight up, and thinking how strange it was that she should be here, and with Simon. "I'll remember."

They were on a gravel road, circling another lake. "Someday we'll pack a picnic and walk over here to Lady Lake. Good fishing here."

She was pleased. That meant he was coming back while she was there. She said casually, "How long can you stay this time?"

He turned the Porsche onto the hard-top. The fir trees seemed to thin out a little, and there were aspen and birch along the roadway now, as well as pines.

"I'll be leaving Sunday, late afternoon sometime." He dug in his jeans pocket and handed her the shopping list. "See if there's something I've forgotten, or anything you need. I split my business—half to my friends in town, half to Echo. There's also a cupboard full of canned goods to fall back on, too."

She looked at the paper in her hand. Eggs, matches, bacon, paper toweling, laundry soap, dog food, batteries, fruit, vegetables, pancake flour, sausage, butter— It went on for two columns. "It looks very complete. What are the candles for?"

"Once in a while we get a summer storm that knocks out the electricity for a couple of hours."

She penciled "stamps" on the bottom of the list and tucked it away in her handbag, for they were crossing over a kind of causeway into town. While Simon looked for a parking spot, she said quickly, "I'm paying for the groceries. That's understood, I hope."

He opened the door on her side and grinned at her.

"I'm serious," she insisted. "It's a matter of pride."

"Come to breakfast," he said quietly.

They ate at the counter of the restaurant, their heels hooked over the foot rail. Simon kept up a running conversation with the proprietor and his wife as he forked fried eggs easy over, hash-browned potatoes, and country sausage.

Carrie was hard of hearing, and Malcolm's voice

boomed all over the room as he repeated things for her. "This here's Miss Jenna Wilson, Carrie. Simon says she's going to be staying out at his place for a while. She's been sick."

Carrie looked her over with interest. "Sick, eh? D'you say *Miss* Wilson?"

She nodded. "Please—call me Jenna." She finished her scrambled eggs and spread jam on the last slice of toast. Carrie poured more coffee.

As they were leaving, she heard Carrie's voice, with Malcolm making sh-ing sounds, and her cheeks burned.

Out on the sidewalk Simon took her by the elbow and turned her to face him. "Spitting mad, aren't you?" he chuckled. "Jenna, they've known me forever. They're just curious. There's not a speck of malice in them." He put out a hand and forced up her chin. "When people get to know you, they scarcely notice the scar. I don't."

She wanted to believe him. But how about Carrie's other comment? *Kinda chunky, ain't she? Not so pretty as Patrice.*

"Let's get going," Simon said. "We have a heap of errands."

He took her to the bank and introduced her to one of the tellers, then they walked up the main street to a small medical center. Jenna liked old Dr. Nicolet, who, after Simon had explained the situation to him, said that he'd be honored to take care of Miss Wilson.

"You keep in touch with me, young lady," the white-haired physician ordered. "I'll be expecting a phone call every other day, weekends and all, and one visit in person every ten days, more frequently if you need it."

On the way home to their woods, laden with things from supermarket, hardware shop, and drug store, Si-

84

mon drove to Echo Station. "It's just a mile from where our dirt road hits the graveled county road," he explained. "On good days, that's just a nice hike. Walking's the best exercise you can do now while your ribs are healing. Later I'll let you take out the boat, and you can ride the bike, but for now it's to be walking only. Agreed? Start with a leisurely stroll along the shore, or up to where the gravel begins. Gradually increase both your pace and the distance. Never overdo."

"Yes, Dr. Fraser."

"Don't be smart."

"Simon, you had *butter* on the list. Do you always get butter, never margarine?"

He had his mouth open to reply and the first words nearly out, when he suddenly clamped up tight as any clam. "Clever, aren't you?" he said a bit stiffly. "Stop fishing."

He led her into Echo's general store *cum* gas station *cum* post office. "Didn't you know that Wisconsin's the dairy state?" he asked innocently.

"It took you long enough to think of that one!" She made a face at him, and a woman customer at the grocery counter watched them, amused.

Besides the grocery section, Echo had a dry goods counter, racks of magazines and paperback books, a meat and dairy cooler, hardware and gardening tools, T-shirts and sun-visor hats, fishing rods and applications for hunting licenses. Four rockers were grouped companionably about a pot-belly stove and a small lending library was housed in the shelves nearby.

Suddenly weary, Jenna sank down in a rocker. "All this and stamps, too?" she asked the attractive brunette who came over to greet them, holding out both hands in welcome.

"Linda, this is my friend Jenna Wilson from Chicago. Jenna—Linda Kittelsen, who operates this emporium. How's business? Even more important, how's Olav?"

Linda tucked her arm in Simon's. "Good to see you back, friend. And a cordial howdy to you, Jenna. Now for the questions: one, business is picking up. Summer's coming and so are the tourists, thank God. Two, Olav's thriving. He's never been happier since—" Her voice trembled. "This was such a good idea, Simon, getting him back in his north country. We can never thank you enough for your help."

She turned to include Jenna in the conversation. "My husband's waiting on a customer. Overalls. Back in the fitting room."

Somewhere to the rear of the store a door slammed and Jenna heard the gliding sound of rubber-tired wheels.

He was one of the handsomest men she had ever seen, a large man with light blond hair thickly flecked with gray, neat blond mustache beneath an aristocratic nose, sea-blue eyes, and a proud lift to his chin.

Linda introduced the man in the wheelchair. "This is my husband Olav."

On their way home again, Jenna took Simon to task. "You should have warned me." Her eyes flashed green fire. "You should have told me before we reached Echo that your friend was crippled for life. A double amputee . . . a man like that . . . "

He said tersely, "One of many casualties of the Vietnam war."

The Porsche turned into their clearing and stopped. Jenna reached back for a grocery bag. "What was Olav before he was wounded? What did he do?"

Simon was abrupt. "Among other things Olav cocaptained the U.S. Olympic Ski Team. His specialty was downhill racing."

"Oh, no—" She leaned heavily on the car.

He lifted the sack from her arms and said, more gently. "I want you resting until lunchtime; we've been gone more than two hours."

She called to him, "Do you like rhubarb?"

Simon glanced up from the pier he was building. The rolled-up sleeves of his blue sweater were soaked, and he moved slowly in the heavy waterproofed waders. "Only in pie."

"I meant pie."

He put both hands down on the plank and challenged her. "Real pie—made from scratch?"

"If I can find a rolling pin in that tangle of utensils in your kitchen cupboard." She stood looking out across the lake. The sky was deep blue with fluffy little clouds reflected in the even deeper blue of the water. Overhead, three large birds passed in flight, their wingbeats fast.

Goldfisch raced to the end of the pier, barking after them as they disappeared over the stand of dark pine and spruce to her left. Simon looked up and reached for the hammer. "Loons."

It was almost five when he finished the pier and came in. The pie was baking in the oven, sending out delightful fragrance. Jenna had slept for an hour and now was sitting cross-legged in the middle of the kitchen floor, sorting one by one through the muddle in the cupboard drawers.

"Smells good. What else are we having besides pie?" He shed his wet sweater and socks by the door and headed for a warm shower. "You're not wearing yourself out, are you?"

"Baked potatoes, fresh asparagus, corn pudding—I thought you'd be hungry after all that work. How shall we fix the fish?"

He shouted through the door. "I'll panfry them outside on the grill."

That was out on the redwood deck facing the lake, she remembered, and began searching for a heavy skillet.

When the shower ceased, she called to him. "I've been looking for thread, but I can't find any."

"Try the sideboard in the living room. I think there's some there, along with a lot of yarn. My mother used to knit."

The sideboard was along the wall opposite the stone fireplace. A nineteenth-century Sheraton reproduction, Jenna hazarded. One that was very skillfully done, made of the dark San Domingo mahogany from those giant tropical trees. Her mother had loved antique furniture, and the Hamiltons possessed a number of fine pieces. She had read about the great cabinetmakers and designers of England, who brought about the golden age of English furniture, and she had spent many hours in a museum workshop. Although she was not expert by any means, she could recognize the delicate inlays of honey-colored satinwood and black-streaked rosewood, the beautiful balance of form in the six-reeded legs of the sideboard table.

The finish on this fine piece was dull, even milky, in places. Jenna examined the medallions and found them regrettably clogged with dust. But inside the left-hand cupboard space she found thirty skeins of natural wool yarn, as well as a ball of blue the same color as Simon's old sweater.

Jenna sat back on her heels and pulled open the sideboard drawers, finding knitting needles, patterns, crochet hooks, embroidery floss, old medical journals, and spools upon spools of thread. She took out the spool of white for which she had been searching and thoughtfully surveyed the living room.

88

Near her was an oval Hepplewhite-style dining table and six handsome shield-back chairs. Mahogany again, but like the sideboard the finish was badly neglected. The delicately fashioned writing desk in the corner nearest the kitchen seemed to be all satinwood. There was little chance of mistaking its mellow honey color. A carving of honeysuckles decorated each graceful round leg.

They were doing the dinner dishes in the pine-paneled kitchen, Jenna washing up and Simon drying silverware and setting dishes and pans to drain, when she thought of the furniture again. Dinner had been delicious, and Simon had eaten a full quarter of the pie.

"I'd forgotten fish could taste so good," she said. "What was it, pickerel?"

"Lake trout. Caught just yesterday. Someone gave Olav more than he could use, and he thought you'd enjoy it." He placed cream and sugar, two cups, and their saucers on a painted tray. "We'll have our coffee before the fire, shall we? Goldfisch is there waiting for us already."

The living room looked beautiful with the lamps lit and the flames flickering in the huge fireplace. The evening was cool, and Simon had closed up the house. "Someday I must get proper curtains for all these windows," he remarked. "Something to draw closed at night."

Jenna sat on the sofa with the tray before her on a low table. She poured out the coffee, added two sugars for Simon. "You have some beautiful pieces of furniture here, Simon."

"Mother's mainly. Family pieces. She was from Connecticut; Dad met her when he was East for college." He vanished into the kitchen and returned, a little sheepish, with a second piece of the rhubarb pie.

89

"This was our summer place, you know, and some of the furniture you see was always here. Mother liked her treasured things around her, and I grew up with them. When my parents died, the town house was sold and I took some of their furniture down to my Chicago apartment and the rest of it came out here. Someday it will grace a home of my own. Meanwhile it's here, there, and everywhere. Take a look in the storage shed sometime—the padlock key hangs in the kitchen—the shed's piled high. So's the bedroom I'm using."

She said drowsily, "I'd wondered. This is a lovely room. Simon, if you leave your blue sweater, I'll mend it for the next time you come. I found your mother's yarn."

"Bedtime," he said firmly, getting up to let the Lab out. "Were you warm enough last night?"

"Oh, yes. And you? You're being much too good to me, Simon. I'm afraid I have your bedroom—"

He shrugged his broad shoulders. "No matter. You're here for one purpose—to get well. And I mean to see that you do."

She said a little stiffly, "Yes, of course. Good night, Simon. It was a lovely day."

He came to her then and placed his hands on her shoulders. "Forgive me. I've said it in such a way that you were hurt, and I'm sorry. Sometimes a man gets lonely, Jenna, and it's too easy then to make a mistake."

Goldfisch was barking, asking to come in. "See you in the morning," Simon said.

Sunlight, slanting through the small bedroom window, touched her face and she awakened, knowing that it was Sunday and Simon's last day. She lay still

90

for a while, the blankets pulled up around her ears, thinking of how it would be when she was alone.

Simon had taught her how to lay a fire in the stone fireplace; he had shown her how to check the pilot light for the gas heating panels. She had candles and flashlight batteries and food enough to easily last a month.

While she did her deep-breathing exercises, she reflected wonderingly that she hadn't thought of Blake or Daphne even once until that very moment. Nor Don . . .

Moreover, she had been happy.

Simon found her in the kitchen frying bacon and making him an omelet. "You should be taking it easy. How are you feeling?"

She whirled around. "Good morning! I didn't hear you. Wonderful, Simon."

"Ribs feel okay? No sharp pains? Did you do your exercises?"

"Yes. No. Yes. Are you hungry? Breakfast's ready. How many pieces of toast?"

He said plaintively, "No pie?"

They ate out on the deck, sitting at the round redwood table, watching the sun streak the lake with silver. Goldfisch chased chipmunks, then came to lie at Simon's feet.

After breakfast they walked through the clearing, where the sun shone down on them, into the dappled light of the woods beyond the cottage. Jenna found a great patch of lily-of-the-valley in bloom, and Simon showed her the different evergreens: the flat scaly-leaved arbor vitae, balsams like small Christmas trees, thickly needled spruces, and the tall pines.

After their walk, Jenna rested for an hour while Simon drove over to visit with the Kittelsens. Then it was lunchtime, time for another rest, another walk in the woods, and shortly after that Simon had to leave.

He said, "I've made a list of all the phone numbers you might need—Dr. Nicolet, Echo Station, the fire brigade, my Oak Park number—and the card is Scotch-taped right by the telephone. Linda hopes you'll call her, as well as walk over frequently, and Nicolet, remember, expects you to check with him every other day. Without fail, Jenna."

She walked with him to the car. "I'll take good care of your cottage, Simon, and I'll take good care of myself. That's a solemn promise. Will you phone the Hamiltons for me and tell them I'll be writing?"

He nodded, tossing in his duffelbag. "I enjoyed the weekend, and the pie was great. I'll phone you, occasionally, just to see how things are going."

"When shall I expect you back?"

He shrugged. "I can't be sure."

Goldfisch jumped in and arranged himself comfortably on the passenger seat.

"Out," ordered Simon.

The Lab looked at him uncertainly, then leaped out. "Stay," said Simon, stroking the dog's head affectionately and then getting into the car. "Stay with Jenna."

They watched until the red lights in the rear dwindled from sight and the sound of the Porsche could no longer be heard, then Jenna fed the Lab and made a cheese sandwich for herself. She ate her supper sitting on a boulder by the lakeshore while the sunset sky flamed rose and gold and faded into twilight.

An hour or so later she was lying in bed, reading a book from the piled assortment on the marble-top table, lost in the old magic of *Little Women*. Goldfisch came to her, padding quietly across the living room to settle himself for the night on a rag rug by her bed.

Presently she turned out the light and went to sleep.

Chapter 6

The alarm clock said six thirty, and Goldfisch's cold nose touching her hand wakened Jenna. She sat up in bed and yawned, stretching a little—experimentally—and winced. But she could move more freely than the week before, she decided.

The Lab shot out of the room for the kitchen and she hurried after him, unlocking the back door, swinging open the screen door, and watching the dog race off through the clearing.

"Do I whistle or shout to make you come back?" she worried out loud. "I should have had a firm word with you before I opened that door, my friend."

She whisked in and out of a warm shower and was dressed in five minutes. The telephone in the bedroom rang while she was in the kitchen measuring Twining's Earl Grey tea into the squat blue teapot, and she rushed back to her room to answer it.

It was Simon.

Jenna sat down on the edge of the bed. "It's only six forty-five. How did you know I'd be awake?"

"I know my dog. Why are you puffing?"

She said indignantly, "I'm not puffing. Well, perhaps just a bit. I hurried in to catch the phone. How was the trip back, Simon?"

"Uneventful. Everything going all right up there?"

"Just fine—that is, if Goldfisch comes back. I let him out just minutes ago, Simon, and he vanished like a streaker into the underbrush."

"No problem . . . he'll be back," Simon said soothingly. "You need to leash him only if you take him into town."

Which was hardly likely, Jenna thought, listening to Simon's deep voice admonishing her again to be lazy and take long rests. "Call Nicolet around ten," he suggested. "He should be back in the office by then."

Goldfisch chose that moment to announce his return. Simon said he could hear the barking all the way to Chicago, and promptly voiced his own good-byes. "Be seeing you in a week or so . . . take care," he said lightly and rang off.

Jenna replaced the receiver and went to let the dog in. "Good boy!" She patted him extravagantly.

It was too beautiful a morning to be inside a moment longer than it took to make the bed, fix a simple breakfast tray, and wander with it down to the pier. A translucent wash of early sunlight filtered through the pines in dappled patterns and gilded the small ripples on the lake. Jenna drank her tea and looked around at her new world.

Little Bay Lake was three quarters of a mile long and about one quarter mile wide. Simon had told her that. Evergreens and birch trees grew close to the shore, and as far as she could see there were no sandy beaches. It would be too difficult to walk along the shoreline, but she conjectured that perhaps there were little roads that sprouted off from the gravel one, like their own small road from their clearing. And Simon had talked about a sandy cove for swimming.

She ate the last of her toast and patted the Lab, who had come to sit beside her on the warm planks, and promised herself that when she felt stronger she was going exploring.

Simon had been a little hazy about neighbors on the lake. He thought some Madison people had bought the log lodge about a quarter mile off to the northeast, and his parents had been friendly with the Parrs, candy-manufacturers from Indianapolis, who lived almost directly across the lake. One could see their lights at night, he said. He surmised that there might be another cottage or two, but they'd be tucked farther back off the water. Privacy was important to the few families who owned land on Little Bay, and that's the way each owner hoped it would stay.

Jenna wondered what it would be like in winter. She pictured herself snowbound, sitting before the huge fireplace while great white drifts made the road impassable. Simon would have to snowshoe in. It would be quiet, but no quieter really than it was this June morning. She realized suddenly that she was lonesome. The Lab came close and lay beside her.

She sat staring straight ahead, with her hands clasped around her knees. "We're both a little lonely, aren't we, Goldfisch?" she admitted.

The day passed slowly. She remembered to check in with Dr. Nicolet, and she did her exercises. Before lunch she and the dog took a short walk in the woods, then in the afternoon she mended Simon's sweater and put it aside to wash the next morning. She took a long nap, fed the dog at four o'clock, and wept over *Little Women*.

There was no time at all to fix her face or do anything about the tear stains when a gray van swept into the clearing. Linda Kittelsen came running up to the door, calling her name.

"I phoned twice and got no answer, so I came myself to be sure you were all right." She reached out and touched Jenna's arm. "Oh my dear, you've been lonely—"

Jenna nodded, unable to answer for a moment. "Have you time for coffee?" she asked, setting out cups, finding spoons.

"You mustn't worry about me, Linda. You're so busy at the store, and I'm getting stronger every day.

Truly. It was that part in *Little Women*—about Beth, remember? And this was my first day alone and I just . . ."

"Let your hair down and wailed?" Linda suggested gently. "I've done it, too."

Jenna's heart thumped. Of course she had.

The other girl was looking at her thoughtfully. "Will you come back with me for supper? Olav's making a Norwegian treat—fish balls and dill potatoes."

It was suddenly important to Jenna that she not leave the cottage, not on this first day alone. It would be running away. She said, "May I say 'thank you but no' and hope to be invited another day?"

Linda put down her empty cup and nodded as if she understood. "That's probably wise of you. The first day in any new situation is always full of little problems, isn't it? And feeling weepy is a large part of convalescence."

She bent down and scratched behind the Lab's ears, and Goldfisch sighed with pleasure. Jenna followed her out of the house and down the little steps to the car. As Linda's van reached the turn in the road, she looked back and waved. "Walk over and see us tomorrow!" she called.

Jenna returned slowly to the house. It was so still, so absolutely quiet. No jungle sound of traffic, not a radio nor a TV blaring. She scrambled eggs, made a small green salad, and took her tray to the wide window seat in the living room.

She ate her supper in the silence, looking out over the lake to catch the first changing colors of the sky. When shadows deepened on the shoreline, she tidied up the kitchen, tended to the dog's needs, and was ready for bed.

* * *

Morning came, bright with a fresh wash of light. Jenna flung the covers back and swung out of bed with new vigor, surprising the Labrador who had just begun to stir.

Yesterday was over. This day was going to be better!

She caught the fragrance of the forest as she stood on the back doorstep letting out the dog, and she went hurrying to the bedroom to find heavier shoes. Young chipmunks scattered in front of her as she started out on the smaller path that trailed off through the woods in a southerly direction.

The air smelled of pine resin and damp earth. She paused on the path in a moist place where there were mosses like green velvet. Nearby bloomed the trefoil beauty of trilliums springing up from a carpet of pine needles, their wavy white petals touched with purple at the base. Wood violets spread their special blue off to one side.

Goldfisch came bounding up, delighted to have company, and loped ahead of Jenna while she explored more slowly along the path. Beside some fallen birch trees she found a bed of ferns and knelt down to examine the young fronds, tightly coiled and covered with thick coatings of pale green fuzz. Her nostrils caught their woodland scent of damp earth and cool water. Dense patches of the distinctive striped foliage of the trout-lily were still visible here and there, but their dainty yellow bell-flowers had already bloomed.

Jenna brushed pine straw and bits of leaf-mold from the front of her slacks and hurried after Goldfisch. The Lab had set up a volley of frenzied barking, and when Jenna rounded a turn in the path she found him in a meadowlike clearing racing around a small shed where two chipmunks had taken refuge from him on the roof.

One of them sat upright on its strong hind legs as

still as a little weathervane on the roof ridge. The other scampered back and forth, peering roguishly over the edge at them, chattering. A jay scolded from the branch of a tree near the little building, and Goldfisch circled around to send a warning bark in its direction.

Jenna examined the door of the small shed. Padlocked. And there were no windows. Jenna wondered if it might be an emergency electrical system for the cottage. Perhaps the Kittelsens would know; she could ask Linda that afternoon.

It was warmer in the clearing, for the mild sunlight could shine straight in. Jenna sank down on a tufty patch of grass and looked up at the serene blue sky. She leaned back against a young sugar-maple tree that was just unfolding its new green, shutting her eyes and listening to the forest noises: the chipmunks' chatter, a robin's call, leaves moving in the slight breeze. The Lab came to sit beside her, panting from his unsuccessful efforts with the chipmunks.

The dog was ready for a drink of water and Jenna was ready for breakfast, but before leaving the clearing she walked once around the little shed—and caught her breath.

In a moist ditch, completely out of sight from the front, marched a row of wild iris. The ditch glowed with color . . . bright green sword-shaped leaves and graceful violet-blue flowers tinged with yellow. She plucked one, carefully, so as not to disturb the plant itself, and saw that the bank on which she leaned held a thicket of shrubs whose leaflets she recognized with delight. This little meadow would soon be bright with the lovely pink of wild roses.

Jenna walked back to the cottage again, content. She was astonished to see that it was already nine o'clock. No wonder she was hungry!

She fried two slices of hickory smoke-scented bacon and popped a frozen waffle in the toaster, made a fresh pot of tea, added an apple to her tray, and carried it into the living room. With paper and pencil at her side, she arranged herself on the sofa before the fireplace and enjoyed her breakfast. Goldfisch snoozed noisily under the sideboard.

An hour later she made a careful list, walking from room to room in the cottage and examining closely the chairs and tables, sideboard and chests. After each piece she placed a mark identifying the condition of the finish.

She found the shed key hanging in the kitchen, just where Simon had said, and caught her breath when she found three black-walnut Belter chairs, candle stands, a tilt-top table, a set of four American Windsors, a child's rocker, an antique crib, and more that she could not safely reach to identify.

The furniture was stacked, piece upon piece, but each was carefully cushioned with folded terry towels and old sheets. Jenna sighed, thinking of the finish, prayed that the shed's roof did not leak, and wondered what the changes in temperature had done to the wood in three years.

Leaving Simon's bedroom until last, she pushed open the door and, feeling like an intruder, stepped in. It would have been a pleasant room, with one window holding a view of the lake and another looking back to the tall evergreens of the forest, if—

" . . . If I could get in," Jenna muttered.

It wasn't quite that bad, of course. Simon had left room for his narrow bed with its simple dark blue spread and log-cabin patchwork quilt folded at the foot, a brown leather armchair and the modern floor lamp beside it, and a handsome Empire chest-of-drawers with lion-mask brasses, which Jenna bent down to examine.

A scrolled pine mirror hung above the dresser, and the picture on the chest's polished surface, she noted with interest, was that of his parents, taken probably some ten years before. The photograph of the beautiful girl was not in sight.

Furniture lined the walls and filled the rest of the bedroom—a Pembroke table piled high with books, a Sheraton sofa with a Queen Anne tea table upended upon it and, in a painted Welsh cupboard, the tea set itself and columns of china, a spoon-turned washstand matching the bed in her room and holding what Jenna suspected was a great deal of very old Waterford crystal.

She took the completed list with her into her bedroom and lay down to rest, frowning over it, studying the possibilities.

One thing was certain. She had found the way to repay Simon, if only a little, for his kindness to her. The two months need not be all resting, reading, and walking, after all.

She retreated back in time, searching her memory to the hours she had spent with Martha Hamilton as a museum volunteer maintaining antique furniture. Carnauba wax, paraffin wax, beeswax . . . a good French polish . . . pumice powder . . . the proper soft cloths. Surely the store at Echo carried turpentine and linseed oil, perhaps even the fine abrasive paper and the artists' brushes she would need. The other items would have to be sent from Chicago.

Jenna reached for her pen and began the letter to Martha Hamilton.

The sun was directly overhead when Jenna and Goldfisch left the dirt road behind and continued on their leisurely way to Echo. High noon by the sun; 1:00 P.M. daylight-saving time. The day had warmed and she unbuttoned her cardigan, took it off, and tied the sleeves loosely around her neck.

She had forgotten her watch and began to laugh because she realized how little it mattered. The Lab, rambling about in the underbrush along the road ahead of her, looked back then and came to trot at her heels. They made a rather stately procession, with Jenna moving a bit stiffly because of the rib-belt.

Only one car passed them, a truck coming from the opposite direction, and the driver leaned out and waved. Jenna shifted the knapsack on her back and lifted her hand in friendly return.

She walked slowly, remembering Simon's advice, and heard birds sing from the treetops and saw a startled young racoon lift its black-masked face, then melt back into the coarse grass along the gravel road. Jenna sighed happily; it really was a beautiful day.

Just off the gently curving road stood Echo Station. Jenna ran up the step and opened the door of the Kittelsens' store, walked with Goldfisch down the middle aisle, groceries on one side and the dry goods counter on the other. "Hello!" she called out.

Linda came from the back, wiping her hands on her gigantic apron. "Hi, we've been looking for you." She glanced shrewdly at Jenna, then grinned. "Better today, aren't you?"

"Oh, much . . . I feel good all over." She hesitated. "I shouldn't have Goldfisch in the store, should I?"

"Well, no, not in the store, but Simon always lets him visit us in the apartment. Olav's there." She called out, and a low whistle from somewhere at the back of the store set the Labrador to trembling. He lifted his head to Jenna and whined.

"All right," she said, "go."

101

"Good heavens," Linda remarked, "I never saw him do that for Patrice—stay at heel, I mean, until released. He's very much Simon's dog, you know. It used to infuriate her to be ignored so by a mere animal."

Jenna perched on a high stool by the grocery counter and watched Linda put together a food order for a lodge a few miles away. "People keep saying the name 'Patrice,' Linda. Who's Patrice?"

Linda weighed out a bag of apples, her hands quick and sure on the scales. "How long have you known Simon?" she countered.

Evidence hung before her eyes. Jenna consulted the large picture calendar on the wall of the store. "A little more than a month." She watched the closed look settle over the other girl's face. "I was in an auto accident early in May," she said. "Simon drove up in his car and helped us. I think he saved my life because I was no longer able to breathe. I'm not trying to pry, Linda."

"No, no, of course not." Linda went on very slowly, "I would not have mentioned her name—Simon has done so much for us, you understand?—and anyway it is not good practice from a business point of view to repeat anything one hears here in the store."

She was troubled, Jenna could see. "It's all right," she assured her. "Forget I asked."

But Linda was not satisfied. "I think in fairness to you I must tell you, or it will be in your mind and grow into something of huge importance. Which it is not."

She was boxing the groceries now, the canned goods first, then the lighter items. "Simon was going to marry Patrice. It was something of an on-again-off-again affair all this last year, however. Simon had begun to seriously consider returning here to practice with old Dr. Nicolet. And Patrice—well, she's the only

102

daughter of the super-wealthy Meadows family. You know, the big department stores all through Illinois and out in California? Well, she wouldn't hear of that! She'd been trying as it was, with little enough luck, to get Simon to go into a professional associates setup right there in Chicago, so he'd have fewer calls at night. And then to have Simon begin thinking about leaving the big city altogether for a rural practice—well, that only heaped more coals on poor Patrice.

"She could never have lived up here, never have let it be so much of her life, as it is his." Linda was emphatic.

"I understand that the whole thing blew up in his face last month. He was telling Olav and me. The Meadows were having a dinner party, May third, I think it was. A big affair—the governor and a senator from California—and Simon never showed up. He tried to explain to Patrice that he'd been with a patient, a little girl who died, but she wouldn't even speak to him."

The screen door banged and Linda stopped talking at once. Jenna stared at the calendar while Linda went off to the dairy fridge to get the milk for the customer. May third . . . the night of her accident—

"Is it over between them?" Jenna asked when they were alone again.

Linda made a wry face. "It seems she's marrying the senator. But who knows? Patrice has changed her mind before."

Jenna could hear Simon's voice. *Sometimes a man gets lonely . . .*

Their conversation lagged. Jenna dug out the letter to Martha Hamilton from her knapsack and dropped it down the mail slot. She wandered over to the hardware section, found the brushes she wanted and a sheet

103

of No. 600 Wet and Dry abrasive paper. She called over to Linda, "Have you turpentine?"

Olav came in with fresh coffee for all of them, and got the turpentine and linseed oil for her. He watched her stow her purchases in the knapsack. "Is there room for some fish I have for you?" he asked. "It's a nice piece of walleye for your supper."

"Walleyed pike. You can fry it," Linda said, seeing her hesitation.

"Oh. I don't know much about fish, their names and all that, but yes, I'd appreciate some walleye. The trout we had Saturday night was so delicious. Thank you, Olav."

She recalled her morning walk and asked, "On Simon's land there's a small shed, away from the house and at the end of a little path. What is it, do you know?"

Olav explained that it was a wash-house. "Automatic washer and dryer—you flick that red switch in the kitchen to turn on the electricity out there." He and Linda had seen it once. "No reason why you should not be using it," he said as she made ready to leave. "Just always remember to turn the electricity off again back in the kitchen when you are finished."

He whistled for the Lab and Goldfisch came loping out of the back apartment straight to Jenna.

A surprised look flickered over Olav's face. "Simon's dog is content to be with you, Jenna."

"No, not really. He's frightfully lonesome for Simon, I can tell. He's decided I'm just his—his responsibility until his master returns."

She remembered then and turned quickly to Linda. "Will you have rhubarb if I walk over on Friday?"

Olav placed his empty coffee cup on the top of the pot-belly stove to refill it with the hot, strong liquid he had brewed. There would be ample pie-plant, he

104

assured her. And bananas, peaches, strawberries, even watermelon. Friday was a good day to come for fruit.

Jenna said hopefully, "Simon might be up for the weekend. He likes pie." She stood very still while Linda adjusted the knapsack on her back. "Thank you for telling me," she said quietly.

Linda nodded. "Don't try to do too much too soon," she cautioned.

Jenna blinked. She reached home with Goldfisch, still not at all certain in which of two ways Linda had meant her last remark.

Three days passed. It was easy to settle into the gentle routine of morning walks in the woods with the Labrador, of long rests on the pier with a pillow beneath her head and another cushioning her right side, of food when she was hungry, and quiet hours with books her mother might have owned: *Anne of Green Gables, The Scotch Twins, Heidi, Swift Fawn, Wind in the Willows.*

Jenna grew stronger and knew that soon she would be discarding the rib-belt completely.

She spent no time consumed with worry, as she had done back in Chicago. Instead, these first hours were filled with the warm contentment of cleaning Simon's kitchen cupboards and putting down fresh shelf paper. When that was completed to her satisfaction, she washed each piece of the old Waterford cut glass in mild soap water with a little ammonia and stored the pieces safely on a clean cupboard shelf until the Sheraton sideboard would be ready to receive them.

On Friday morning she walked again to Echo, visited with her new friends, and came home with rhubarb for a pie and fresh milk for the tea. After a rest she tidied the cottage, remade both beds with fresh sheets, and did her baking.

105

She explained to Goldfisch, "He can't get here any earlier than midnight, you know. More likely one or two, even." But they were ready by seven, with a fire laid just as Simon had shown her, and the oval Hepplewhite table set with dark-red linen placemats and napkins, the white Wedgwood plates from the kitchen, and sparkling Waterford goblets. In the center of the sideboard was a cut-glass vase with a single splendid wild iris.

She had made herself take an extra long afternoon rest, falling asleep with her finger keeping the place in *Heidi*, so that she could be awake when he came. At eleven she lit the kindling, standing back to see the fire race through the wood shavings and become bright tongues of flame that hissed and leaped in the firewood.

Goldfisch came out of her bedroom and resettled himself on the Navajo rug in front of the wide hearth. Jenna selected knitting needles and a pattern from the sideboard and cast on the first stitches in natural wool to begin an Irish-fisherman sweater for Simon.

The fire blazed; the dog slept; and Jenna knit.

At two o'clock she roused the Labrador and walked with him in the night darkness to the edge of the clearing. From the top branches of a tall balsam came the soft hooting sound of an owl. Goldfisch bounded out of the woods again and they walked together back to the kitchen door.

Jenna checked the fire screen, put away the pie, and disconnected the electric coffee pot. It was time for bed, and Simon had not come.

Loneliness flooded back on Saturday when she stirred and opened her eyes. She made tea and took a short walk with the dog.

106

"Any mail for me?" she asked when Linda telephoned to hear if Simon had come.

No mail. No answer yet to her letter to Martha. The Kittelsens invited her to come for Sunday noon dinner with them and promised to drive her home later.

Still hopeful that Simon would arrive, she defrosted a pot roast, scrubbed potatoes and carrots so they would be ready to cook. Much of the afternoon she spent carefully washing the satinwood writing desk, little by little, with a weak solution of lukewarm water and mild Ivory soap. She worked slowly, removing all dirt and grease from the surface, but never allowing the wood itself to become wet.

It would have been nice to work outside in the clear bright light, she reflected, but that was obviously not possible. She still was not to do any lifting. Instead, she spread newspapers on the living-room floor and sat on a little stool when she tired of kneeling.

She was pleased with the result of her efforts. The actual finish on the desk had not been damaged during the years of neglect, so the next step could be the polishing. That must wait, however, until the materials she had requested arrived from her friend in Chicago.

Next she would work on the sideboard. And *that* would probably be quite another story!

The telephone rang at ten thirty Sunday morning, and Jenna, who was doing dishes, dived for it and said "hello" breathlessly, for her side hurt a little from hurrying.

Breathlessly but hopefully, too. Only it wasn't Simon.

"Did you bump into something?" Linda asked, all concern. She was calling to remind Jenna to bring her knitting when she came for dinner. "I'm coming over to pick you up."

Jenna gathered her things together slowly, feeling a reluctance to leave the cottage. What if Simon should come, wet and out of sorts from a long drive in the rain? It was no welcome for a weary man—an empty house, a cold hearth.

Later, she was glad she had gone, for of course Simon had not come while she was away—it was Sunday, after all. And the Kittelsens were good company. Olav showed her how to make the creamed dill potatoes that they had, along with baked trout, new asparagus, and cherry cobbler. They sat together around a table in their small kitchen, with a high school boy in to tend store for two hours to give them their brief Sunday break.

Afterwards they sat awhile in the little parlor, Goldfisch sprawled on one side of the wheelchair and Linda close on the other, sitting cross-legged on the floor with Olav's hand gently stroking her brown hair while she laboriously tackled the knit-one-purl-one of a beginner's knitting.

Jenna bent her head over the intricate blackberry stitch of the fisherman sweater. She asked, "Did you know Simon before, when he was growing up here?" and Olav smiled.

"We were in high school together."

"You, too, Linda?"

Linda dropped her knitting in her lap and reached up to hold her husband's hand. "No, I'm Texas-born. I met Olav in Houston. I was teaching in a suburban elementary school near the hospital to which he came after he was flown back from Vietnam."

She lamented, "Can you imagine a teacher being so stupid about learning how to knit? Now what have I done wrong?"

"Dropped some stitches," Jenna guessed, taking the blue yarn thrust at her.

Linda mourned, "After three girls, my sister hopes for a boy, but at this rate he'll be in kindergarten before I finish the baby sweater." She rose gracefully to her feet. "Talk with Olav awhile, Jenna, while I relieve Benny."

An hour later it was time for Jenna to leave. "I can walk back," she insisted. "It will do me good after that wonderful meal."

But Linda would not hear of it and on their way home to Simon's cottage, she explained to Jenna, "Next time you see Olav he will probably be back on his artificial legs and crutches—his posts and sticks, he calls them. There are times, you know, Jenna, when stumps develop a soreness and then he must use his chair, which he despises. He is a proud man, Jenna—"

Jenna hopped out of the van and the Lab leaped out after her. "I had a lovely time, thank you. You're pretty wonderful people, you know," she said quietly. "Both of you."

Linda looked far off into the rain-gray sky. "We were lucky to find each other, Olav and I." Her brown eyes softened with the thought. She said, "You're all right, Jenna? You'll not be too lonely, even with this rainy weather?"

There were a hundred things to do, Jenna assured her. No time to be lonesome. "It will be sunny tomorrow. Thanks again!" she called as the van swung down the little dirt road.

She fed the Lab and knit two rows of pattern on Simon's sweater. Then she wrote letters, enclosing a short note to Blake and Daphne in her weekly letter to the Hamiltons. It sounded prosaic and stuffy, she thought, and she frowned over it, feeling strands of worry begin to edge their way into her mind. She wondered how they were managing, her sister and brother . . .

Hastily she sealed the envelope, then took a long, warm shower and shampooed her hair.

Raindrops still streamed on the bathroom window panes as she put her hair up in rollers. She shivered and reached for her warm flannel robe. It would be a good night for an open fire. Or for reading in bed.

She opted for the latter, slipping her feet into the fluffy sheepskin slippers and going into Simon's room to choose a book from the pile on the pretty Pembroke table. By eight o'clock she was in bed, feeling ridiculously comfortable with a cup of hot tea and a fine old leather-bound copy of Scott's *Lady of the Lake*.

"It takes little to please you," Simon had said to her once and she thought about that for a moment, wondering sleepily if it were true.

Somewhere near midnight she heard the dog's throaty whine and came awake, speaking soothingly to the Lab and groping for the lamp switch. Light glowed in the room, shone on rain-streaked windows. Goldfisch raised his head, ears cocked.

Her heart thumped. "What is it, boy?"

The dog barked and trotted off to the kitchen and Jenna reached for her robe.

Goldfisch was at the back door, excitedly begging to be let out. She hesitated, flashlight in hand, and then she saw headlights. A car swept into the clearing, and the dog went wild.

Jenna opened the door and stepped out on the little landing to welcome Simon back home, and the Lab raced forward with joyous barks.

Simon was wearing brown slacks and a cream turtle-neck knit shirt. A thrust of wind-driven rain soaked his shoulders and wet his dark hair. "What a night for driving!" he said, grinning at her.

110

He had a watermelon under one arm and a grocery bag balanced on the other. "The rest of the stuff can wait until morning," Simon said, putting things down on the kitchen table, and bending to quiet the dog, caressing him roughly with his large tanned hands.

"But it's Sunday," Jenna declared, still astonished to see him. "Monday almost." She asked, "Tea or coffee?" and Simon shook his head.

"Scotch and water." He said wearily, "Stand still. Let me look at you."

One hand clutching the teakettle, she turned to face him, hating the hair rollers and the old bathrobe and the scar on her cheek.

"I feel fine," she said, but Simon continued to stare at her.

After a long moment he asked, "Can you sleep in those things?" He came to her and pulled the rollers out, one by one, and the pins fell all over the kitchen floor.

"I've missed you," he said, almost angrily.

She had missed him, too, but there was no point in telling him that. She stammered, "I—I made you a rhubarb pie on Friday."

"Good," he said, "I'll have it for breakfast."

But pie crust gets soggy if it is not eaten when it should be, and she told him indignantly, "You didn't come . . . I had to give it to the chipmunks."

Too late she remembered Patrice and her complainings.

Simon's dark eyes grew icy. "I *couldn't* come," he said tersely. "Go to bed, Jenna—we're seeing Nicolet in the morning."

"I will not be sent off to bed as if I were a naughty child!" Her green eyes sparked with indignation. "I'm sorry if I sounded bitchy, truly I am. I didn't mean to be, Simon." Her voice wavered, "It's wonderful to see

111

you. I—I've been a little lonesome, and you didn't call—"

Oh dear, that sounded like another complaint, she thought. Better that she did take herself off to bed at that rate. "Your bed's made up fresh, Simon. While you take a warm shower, I'll turn it down for you." Her voice trailed off, and she looked anxiously at him.

He was standing at the door to his bedroom, Goldfisch at his feet. And he was smiling. "Speech over?" he asked her, amused. "I'm sorry, too. I came on a little strong there . . . just tired. It's been a hard week, Jenna, and a long drive up here alone."

"Come here," he said softly.

He reached out and pulled her gently into his arms. Carefully . . . not hurting her right side. He smiled down at her. "I missed you," he said again, wonderingly.

He put his hand under her chin and lifted her face up to his, and his lips touched hers, gently at first, then with a fierceness that took her breath away.

She felt joy, and a sweet peace. Her head rested against his broad chest, close to his heart, and she heard Simon say, "Do you know what would be a good idea?"

Something in his voice made her tremble, and his hands closed on her shoulders, hard, while he searched her green eyes for his answer.

She heard the echo of his voice, *Sometimes a man gets lonely and it's easy then to make a mistake . . .*

And it would be a mistake. She knew that as certain as she was standing there, warm against him, wishing it could be different—

"No," she said firmly, and his dark eyebrows soared.

He asked, "No?" and she leaned back as far as she could, away from the disturbing length of him.

"Are you sure you know what I was going to suggest?" He traced her mouth with his index finger, smiling at her confusion.

"I—I think so, Simon. But when—when people are lonely, they might do things they regret—later."

"Little innocent," he murmured and let her go.

She felt adrift, abandoned. Alone . . .

"Friends?" she asked seriously.

With a wry grin he leaned down and dropped a light kiss on her uptilted nose. "Friends," he assured her. "And *now* go to bed before I change my mind."

Chapter 7

In the morning when she awakened it might all have been a dream, except that no Lab slept on the floor at the foot of her bed and from the kitchen came breakfast sounds.

Jenna dressed hastily, scrambling into blue jeans and a white blouse with little green-embroidered scallops around the collar, brushing out her hair and frowning at the tangles. Remembering . . .

Simon was whistling. "Two sausages?" he asked, breaking off and looking at her.

She felt blood rush warmly to her cheeks.

Simon grinned. "Can't think when I've last seen a maiden's blushes," he teased her, flipping the sausages over. His hand slid into hers. "Good morning, friend. You fix the toast."

It was still too wet to eat down on the pier, and they settled for the table in the living room. Simon touched the Waterford goblet at his place. "Busy fingers?" He looked interested.

Jenna rushed to explain. "Oh, you don't mind, do

you, Simon? It would give me such pleasure." Her hands clutched each other, tense in her lap.

Simon said, "I think I have something for you."

He came back from the Porsche with a box in his arms. "It begins to make sense—all that wax."

"From the Hamiltons?" She was ecstatic.

Simon shrugged. "With love from Martha. Her exact words. Hey," he yelled at her, "finish your breakfast first!"

She came back from the bedroom, bringing her list to the table and showing him, between bites of toast and egg and sausage, what she planned to do. "If I may," she said, eager now for his approval.

He was a little intrigued, Jenna could tell.

"I know what to do," she assured him. "The museum taught us, you see, and I'd use only the right materials, Simon, and the really proper techniques. I'm not talking about *stripping* down to bare wood, you know." She shuddered. "Not like those awful places that take lovely old pieces like these of your mother's and strip right through everything down to the raw wood with all the grain opened up. I plan mainly to restore the polish."

She put down her fork and challenged him. "Well, may I?"

He shrugged. "You seem to know what you're talking about. Only—"

She interrupted, "Oh, Simon, thank you. I promise I shan't touch a piece that I'm not sure about."

He continued, " . . . Only, no lifting."

Her mouth opened slightly in protest. "Not now, of course, but maybe in a month or so?"

He grunted, "Stop wheedling. No lifting until explicit permission has been granted. Finished eating? Let's walk the dog."

114

He was looking at her quizzically, and wisely she said nothing more.

Jenna fetched her cardigan and Simon went to get his blue pullover, and she watched his face when he first saw the mending.

"Clean, too," he marveled and came to her, thanking her with a gentle hug. "Don't change my life too much, hyacinth-girl," he warned.

There was a tenderness in his voice, so she decided that it didn't really matter that she did not understand the words.

They went down the steps off the redwood deck and to the lake, standing on the shore to watch the water, which was as still after the storm as a length of blue silk. Early sunshine warmed their faces.

"You haven't asked about Blake or Daphne," Simon said.

She bent to choose a flat pebble and sent it skipping in the lake and the ripples widened and widened, reaching all the way back to the rocks on which they stood.

"No, I haven't. I knew you'd tell me, Simon." She looked up at the arch of rain-washed sky above them. "Sometimes I don't understand myself," she admitted. "I don't want to even think about things back home for then I start to worry, really *worry*, and this is a little haven, Simon, and I don't want it spoiled. By my worrying, I mean."

Her throat tightened. "It doesn't make sense, does it?"

For a moment there was a sort of satisfied look on Simon's face, and she wondered what it meant, but then it was gone.

He touched her arm, guiding her away from the shore and onto the path she had explored with Gold-

115

fisch a few days earlier. The bushes along the way were all moisture-laden and when the Lab touched the lower branches, myriads of waterdrops sprayed out.

"Blake looked me up last Tuesday," Simon said and Jenna held her breath. "He insisted on knowing where you were—claimed his rights as head of the family, you might say. To make a long story considerably shorter, I asked him if your bills—three months of them—were to come to him, then, as head of the family."

He stopped speaking because Jenna had made a sad little sound.

"Are you okay?" he asked and she cast anguished eyes at him.

Simon fixed his gaze on Goldfisch, rambling ahead in the canine version of seventh heaven, for his master had come home and there were chipmunks to chase. Simon said, "Allow him the privilege of growing up, Jenna."

She turned to him. "But are they all right? Really all right, Simon?"

"No new problems. The Cutlass has been exchanged for a small Dodge, I believe. Parker Hamilton has his eye out for them both, Jenna. He told me to assure you of that."

They had reached the little clearing and she showed him the stately line of wild iris and told him about the chipmunk that had stayed still as a weathervane atop the shed roof.

"Olav says there's a washer-dryer in the shed. May I use it?"

Simon explained about the kitchen switch and then looked at his watch. "Time to get you dressed for town," he said. "Nicolet expects us at eleven for your ten-day checkup."

116

She thought of the days he hadn't called and asked him bluntly, "You've been in touch with Dr. Nicolet?"

His voice was bland. Plainly that was none of her business. "Wear something easy to get in and out of," he said. "There'll be X rays."

They walked back to the cottage, alongside the tall pines with their endless dripping after the night's rain, and Jenna took a shower and dressed in a blue blouse and a wrap-around blue denim skirt. She thrust her feet into blue Bernardo sandals, caught up her purse and her white cardigan sweater, and was ready.

Simon had changed into dry slacks and moccasins. He looked at her and whistled. "Powder your nose and let's go!"

She froze, her eyes brimming with hurt.

He gave her a startled look. "What did I say? For God's sake, Jenna, what is it?"

"The scar—"

"What about it?"

"You said 'powder your nose.' What you really meant was 'cover up the scar,' wasn't it?"

Simon seized her shoulders, then cradled her head against him. Protectingly. She caught the clean, clean smell of him. "You've been hurt too much, too often. Damn it, Jenna, that scar's coming off!"

She pulled away from him. "Sorry. I just thought . . . " She broke off.

"You think too much," he said, and seized her hand. "Come on or we'll be late."

The neat secretary-nurse took her name and vanished through the door. Simon sat in a far corner, thumbing nervously through ancient magazines. Jenna picked up her handbag and followed the girl, who had returned and beckoned to her.

With a friendly nod, Dr. Nicolet indicated a chair.

117

He bent again to her folder. From the corner of her eye, Jenna caught movement in the corridor to her left, and saw a small red-haired girl staring in at her.

Jenna smiled and wiggled her fingers, but the child did not move an eyelash. Then the little girl's mother came along and said, "So there you are, Beth—"

An unusual voice . . . so flat, lifeless . . . without hope? Jenna sat there, appalled.

Dr. Nicolet repeated his question and she turned, hastily, to respond. Later there were X rays, and the old physician called Simon in, and the two of them studied the dripping films, talking quietly together.

On the way home she asked him, "Everything's coming along fine, isn't it? You both said it was. So why do I need to wear the rib-belt one more week?"

It was precautionary, Simon explained. "To remind you to be a good girl," he said, his dark eyes alive with amusement.

She considered that. "How long can you stay?" she asked.

He let out a great whoop of laughter. "I trust the two items of conversation aren't related," he said.

She was embarrassed. "You *know* I didn't mean—"

His eyebrows shot up. "What? What didn't you mean?"

She turned her head to the window, chin up high, refusing to answer, and he laughed and then said, seriously, "Tuesday morning. I've covered my calls until that evening. Would you like to drive a little?"

She stiffened and shook her head. "I—I couldn't," she said uneasily.

The Porsche reached the gravel road and they turned off toward Echo Station. Simon said casually, "Olav tells me the Lab obeys you very well."

So he had telephoned Olav, too. Olav . . . Dr. Nicolet . . . why not her? She felt miffed and tried not

118

to show it, for a bleak look had settled down over Simon's face.

When they were back at the cottage, Jenna unpacked the few items she had purchased at Echo and set about making the rhubarb pie for supper. Simon took out his fishing equipment and disappeared with the dog, coming back late in the afternoon, quite uncommunicative.

Jenna served dinner and they ate almost in silence. When it was time for dessert, she excused herself and went to the kitchen, returning a bit later with the coffee tray and the pie, neatly quartered, each piece bearing a tiny, toothpicked flag. The flags said: EAT ME; EAT ME, TOO; EAT ME IF—; and EAT ME AND BE SORRY.

Very solemnly she poured his coffee, added two sugars, served him EAT ME, and marched quietly into her bedroom, closing the door firmly behind her.

She heard laughter, then there was a knock on the door. She sniffed. Two could play at this game.

The knocking grew more insistent. "Jenna? Jenna, come out." Then, "Do you hear me, girl? Please come out and share this beautiful pie."

Silence. She heard a drawer pulled open. Then the doorknob turned ever so slightly and Goldfisch edged in, trotting over to her with a small white envelope tied loosely around his neck. She reached down and withdrew the message.

On one side of the flower-embellished card was the greeting: BEST WISHES FROM ALL OF US ON YOUR BIRTHDAY. The card was signed, "Aunt Lu, Uncle Bob, and the children."

On the back, Simon had written: "Dear Alice, I never finished reading *Through the Looking Glass*. What do I do now to say I'm sorry? Please come back

119

and eat the pie with me. P.S. This is the only paper I can find quickly. I have no Aunt Lu; is she yours?"

She opened the door and he was there, his hand raised to knock again. "I was going to try once more, then knock it down. Figuratively speaking, of course."

He apologized. "Sorry, I was such a bear. There's been something on my mind . . . "

She laughed a little, shakily. "Is the pie good? I had an Uncle Bob once, but no bears in my family tree and no Aunt Lu."

"That still leaves the children to be accounted for," he said. "The pie's great, only I haven't eaten any yet. I'm waiting for you."

Simon had built a fire of birch and balsam logs and their special fragrance drifted through the house. Outside, a soft dusk fell and a lopsided moon rose over the clearing. A few stars came out.

Jenna switched on a lamp and picked up her knitting. She heard the distinctive four hoots of their owl, and Goldfisch raised his head. He trotted out to the kitchen, then came back to lie at Simon's side.

Simon held a medical journal in his hand, but he had not turned a page for an hour. Jenna thought he might be sleeping, for his head was back, but he reached out a long arm and patted the Lab so she knew he was awake and staring at the ceiling.

"You're a restful person, hyacinth-girl."

Jenna wasn't arguing about that. "You mean 'usually.' "

"Restful," she heard him say again.

A log fell with a soft thud and sparks flew up. Simon said, "Remember the woman you pulled out of the car that night? She's done very well. The child, too, though of course he had no real injuries."

She was delighted. "I'm so glad to hear that. Simon,

shall I put the kettle on? Would you like a cup of tea?"

He looked directly at her. "With another piece of rhubarb pie? You're spoiling me, Jenna."

She set the things out for him on the low, drop-leaf sofa table. "It's you who has done the spoiling," she said earnestly. "Letting me come to this beautiful place . . . "

He polished off the pie, set the plate down, and picked up the teacup and saucer. "I'll be taking your X rays back to Randall. I think he'll be pleased with the progress so far."

She was puzzled. "And Dr. Nicolet?"

"For you he's acting as Dr. Randall's consultant. You're in his charge while you're up here."

"I see." She really didn't, but if he said so, it must be exactly right. Her trust in Simon was immeasurable.

He looked pensive. "John Nicolet's gotten old, Jenna. He's had a heart condition for some years, too."

She thought how difficult it must be for the old physician. Family practice included obstetrics, didn't it? And babies seldom arrived at convenient times—"Couldn't he take in a partner? Some younger man who likes the area? Someone who would gradually take over the responsibilities? That would be the wise thing, wouldn't it, Simon? Imagine what it's like for him in winter!"

A look almost of pain was on Simon's handsome face. "He's saved a place for me all these years. My father was his younger partner, Jenna. The two of them were always so certain I'd come back."

He got up from the wing chair and walked to the front of the cottage, resting one knee on the wide window seat and looking out at the lake. "Lights across

121

the water," he said, thoughtfully. "At the place the people from Madison bought three years ago."

There was the sound of rain falling gently on the roof, spattering against the windows nearest the lake. Simon turned away.

Jenna looked up from her knitting. "Did you notice the little girl in the doctor's office this morning, Simon?"

"The little red-head?" He crossed to the sideboard. "Benedictine?" She shook her head and he poured the golden liqueur into only one of the tiny, fragile glasses. "Yes, I saw her. Why do you ask?"

"I'm not quite sure." She thought about it a few seconds and then said, "It was her mother's voice. Yes, that was it, Simon. It held such unhappiness, I thought."

"That could well be."

"Oh, do you know her? I saw her in Echo one day, but she spoke only to Olav and he didn't introduce her to me. She seemed interested in getting her things and getting out again as fast as possible. Linda didn't mention who she was, and I did not ask."

He would discuss it no further, however, and Jenna picked up the wool and her needles. "When must you leave tomorrow?"

He had his hands locked in back of his head and was watching the logs burn down. She switched off the lamp and they sat, silent, in the fire-lit room.

"Rather early," he said at last. "I must talk to Nicolet. I've been putting it off— No, not about you," he said hastily, for she had startled.

Jenna nodded. "I understand. About the problem that's been on your mind all week."

"*All week!* My God, it's been with me three years now."

122

She looked squarely at him. "So what are you going to do?"

He groaned. "I don't know yet, Jenna. I just don't know."

It seemed an imposition to offer advice. She had needed so much help herself in dealing with her own recent problems. Still—

"My father once said to me, when he was deeply concerned about a troubling case in which he was involved, that a problem was seldom purely either or, but often included dealing with what was best, as well as with what was right. Could you approach your problem that way?" she asked him.

Simon looked at her for a long moment. "You're quite a girl, Jenna," he said, and she flushed.

"Tell me," he asked, and she knew that the question was a real one, "if you loved someone, could you give up a home you liked, friends you enjoyed, and go to live in a strange place, a small town far from the theater and the opera and the great restaurants and all the exciting shops—just to be with the man you loved?"

She swallowed hard on the lump in her throat. "Oh, yes."

"You know for sure, just like that? No thinking it over—no weighing up the balances of pro and con?"

She looked at him, with the light from the fire flickering on his face, and knew that if someone like Simon asked her, she would go anywhere, anytime. But this was strictly a rhetorical question he was posing, not a romantic one for the two of them. So she told him, as honestly as she could: "I'd need three seconds, Simon—one to say yes and the other two to pack a suitcase."

It was said with humor and she laughed a little when she finished, but Simon sat very still. His face clouded and he said grimly, "I fell in love with the wrong girl then."

He left very early Tuesday morning and after the sound of the Porsche died away, Jenna sat on a large boulder near the pier and watched white birds wheel and soar in the tender blue sky. Goldfisch lay on the pier with his head down and sulked.

"Never mind," she comforted him, scratching his ears. "You're not the only one, you silly dog. I miss him, too."

She planned her day. Some exploring first, while the morning was still new. A letter to Martha while she rested, and then, in the afternoon she would make the polish.

The thought of the waxes and of starting work on the sideboard was exciting. She was eager to begin, but Dr. Nicolet had explained all over again to her how important it was that she walk each day and breathe deeply as she walked, so she returned to the cottage for a sweater. Goldfisch saw her start for the clearing and came running after her.

The path to the northeast this time, she decided. She had been a little way along it with Simon that one Sunday. Today was the day she would really explore.

The pine-straw path led straight from the clearing into the woods on one side of the cottage. Here the air smelled of sunshine on evergreen branches and in a small break in the woods she found masses of fragrant lily-of-the-valley, late blooming here for it was mid-June, but reminding her all over again of childhood springtime gardens.

She walked on, smelling the sweetness of the woods, with Goldfisch beside her. Presently the path left the tall pines and slanted eastward across a meadow in the general direction of the lake.

Jenna hesitated, then set off through the springy

124

grass, walking as briskly as her right side allowed. The sun's warmth caught her in dazzling brightness. She heard the clear, flutelike song of a meadowlark.

The ground was soggy from the recent rain. In places it was slippery. Her slacks were soon wet at the ankles. The Lab raced ahead, barking enthusiastically, then loped back to join her slower progress. Beyond the meadow she saw the shimmer of Little Bay Lake and felt a special wonder lift her spirits.

Ahead of them was a rickety fence with an old-fashioned stile for climbing over. And on the other side of the fence was a small red-haired child.

The little girl stood motionless, watching a dragonfly come to rest on a tall reed. Jenna waited until she was closer, then she called, "Hello!"

The child looked up, twisting a bit of meadow grass in her grubby little fingers, and turned to run away. One small foot slipped sideways. She fell easily and the ground was soft, but to Jenna's dismay the child lay motionless.

Awkwardly, Jenna climbed over the stile and hurried to the small figure, kneeling in the damp grass at her side, and asked anxiously, "Are you all right? Did you hurt yourself when you fell?"

Goldfisch came bounding back, his tail wagging an offer of friendship. Jenna saw the child's eyes dart to the dog, so she sat down in the damp grass and called the Lab to her, stroked his bright coat and talked to him. "Can you get up now, Beth?" she asked a bit later and reached to help her.

There was mud down the front of the child's slacks and sweater, and Jenna brushed it futilely. "It will come off better when it's dry. Right now we'll only make it worse. Shall I walk home with you? Do you live nearby?"

Beth offered her hand, silently stealing little glances

125

up at Jenna, and the two of them, with Goldfisch at heel, crossed the meadow together.

Jenna heard the woman calling before she came into view. She looked down at the child. "Don't you want to run ahead, Beth? I can't walk very fast yet because I hurt my side."

Beth's small hand clung more tightly.

The lodge was built of varnished logs on the very edge of the meadow, tucked into the first stand of pines on a little knoll that overlooked the lake. The water-facing windows had a deep overhang to cut the glare of the afternoon sun, and the wide deck jutting out from what appeared to Jenna to be the living room looked like an ideal summer sunning spot. No wonder they could see the lights from Simon's cottage—this gorgeous place practically floated on the water just around the little bend that formed the meadow.

"Hello!" Jenna called to the tall slender woman who was watching them approach. "I found Beth, or she found me—I'm not sure which."

The child dropped her hand and went running to her mother, hiding her face in the woman's smock and peeping shyly out at the visitors.

"I'm Jenna Wilson and this dog answers to the improbable name of Goldfisch, spelled with a 'c' for his place of birth, I understand. Sorry Beth is so muddy. She slipped in the meadow, but I don't think she's harmed herself."

"I'm Megan Adams. Won't you come in and have coffee while I get clean clothes on my youngster? She scooted out while I was doing some laundry just a moment or so ago. That meadow fascinates her."

"What a darling kitchen! You collect the Royal Copenhagen Christmas plates, don't you? They're gorgeous exhibited like that."

126

Mrs. Adams buttoned Beth into clean corduroy slacks and tousled the child's hair lovingly. She poured coffee, looking up at the plate rail as she passed milk and sugar. "Yes, it is nice, isn't it? We remodeled the kitchen when we bought the place three years ago."

She came back to the table where Jenna was sitting and joined her.

Megan Adams was painfully thin, a light brunette with haunted hazel eyes. She was obviously pregnant. Jenna hadn't noticed it at Echo, but then the woman had been wearing a bulky coat.

"When is your baby due?" she asked. "I suppose you're hoping for a brother for Beth."

The woman winced. "That would be nice. The baby's expected toward the end of September."

Jenna finished her coffee. "I'm staying in the Fraser cottage. Do you know the place? Across the meadow and about, oh, I'd guess perhaps a quarter of a mile more through the woods. There's a path—"

Megan Adams shifted uneasily in the kitchen chair.

Jenna couldn't help wondering what was worrying her. "I'd love to have you walk over and visit me," she finished a little hesitantly. "I've got a summer project going, restoring the polished finish on some of Dr. Fraser's antique furniture. I'm usually always home."

She refused a second cup of coffee and walked slowly to the door with Mrs. Adams. "I'm all alone at the cottage. Please come over, sometime when you feel like a walk. You and Beth."

Megan Adams shook her head. "I'm not doing much visiting these days, but thank you, Miss Wilson. It's nice to know there's someone close by."

Thanks but no thanks. Jenna felt a bit embarrassed.

"Beth's made friends with the Labrador," she said, indicating the back step. Goldfisch sat quietly, tolerating the child's closeness. His splendid head was held high; his eyes watched for Jenna.

Megan Adams looked puzzled. "That's quite unusual for her."

"Goldfisch misses Dr. Fraser," Jenna said sympathetically. "He's a very gentle dog. Perhaps you'd let Beth come sometime to keep him company? I'd see that she got safely home again."

The child's mother nodded. "Thank you. Goodbye," she said, "it was nice to meet you."

At the beginning of the woods Jenna looked back. The little girl and her mother both stood in the doorway now, watching. Jenna waved and saw Mrs. Adams lift her hand.

"Well," she commented, happy to be going back to Simon's friendly house, "that was not exactly a successful visit, was it, Goldfisch? Too bad . . . it would have been pleasant to have neighbors."

As soon as she reached the cottage, she got out the hot plate and extension cord that Simon had shown her. It was always safer to melt wax in the open and she could use the covered electrical outlet by the back porch, he had said, warning her to be very careful because waxes easily ignited.

She worked in worn jeans and an old blue shirt of Simon's, placing four parts of carnauba wax, four parts of paraffin wax, and two parts of beeswax together in a large metal pan and, with great care, slowly dissolved the flammable waxes over low heat. She had brought her lunch outside too, and she sat on the little stool watching the hot plate, eating cottage cheese and honey, and finishing with a crisp green Granny Smith apple.

When the waxes had melted, she removed the pan from the heat and set it carefully aside. Then she put the hot plate back in the kitchen and let Goldfisch out again. Cautiously, she added to the liquefied waxes twice the amount by volume of turpentine and stirred the mixture with a wooden spoon while it cooled. The solvent pulled the different waxes together into a single product that flowed smoothly into the can that Simon had found for her.

Only when the wax was completely cool and had set to a hard-paste consistency did Jenna attach the tight-fitting cover.

It was just about then, when she had finished making her paste wax and had lain down with the check list of the furniture in her hand, that Jenna realized what had been niggling away at the back of her mind for the last two hours.

Beth had not talked at all—not once during all the time had she spoken. Not to Jenna, not to the dog, and not even to her mother.

Jenna closed her eyes, thinking. The little girl was five at least, probably almost six. She thought of the way the little hand had reached up to hers, trustingly. Welcome or not, she resolved to walk with Goldfisch up to the Adams' lodge quite soon again.

A few days later she was in the clearing by the back entrance, washing the dust and grease from a pair of walnut candle stands—lightweight items so she was breaking no promises by carrying them from the shed. Goldfisch lifted his head, barked once, and trotted off.

Beth came running out of the woods and the dog leaped to greet her. "Careful, Goldfisch!" Jenna called out. She watched the child and the Lab meet and knew there was no problem there.

Mrs. Adams came along the path, moving more slowly. "Have we come to call at a bad time?" she asked.

"No, indeed, and I'm so glad to see you." Jenna pulled up a lounger. "Will this be comfortable for

129

you? Beth won't want to sit, at least for a while, I can see."

Megan looked at her appealingly. "Will you forgive my earlier coolness? I've forgotten how to make friends, I'm afraid."

Jenna beamed at her. "But you've come—how kind of you. I get a bit weary of my own company just about this time every day."

She explained what she was doing with the candle stands, and took Megan Adams to the living room to see the beginning work on the sideboard and to admire the satinwood desk. "I've done the first coat of wax on the desk. Before I return to Chicago sometime in August, I want to have all this furniture done for Simon. Cleaned, polished, and waxed, I mean."

"What a charming piece this is." Mrs. Adams bent down a little to admire the desk. "It must be awkward to work at it here in the corner though." She indicated the newspapers Jenna had placed around to protect the rug as she worked.

Jenna said, "It is somewhat, but I'm learning to make do. I can't lift yet—not for another month, they tell me. I was in an auto accident."

She saw the woman's expression and added hastily, "I'm fine now—getting stronger every blessed day. It's so lovely a place in which to convalesce, isn't it? But until the ribs are all knit back in shape and there's no chance at all of the lung collapsing again, I follow doctor's orders."

They had their tea out on the redwood deck, watching afternoon shadows turn the lake to the iridescent turquoise color of a Mexican butterfly's wing. Jenna knit and Beth fed cooky crumbles to an ever-willing Goldfisch. Mrs. Adams sat quietly resting.

At four o'clock she said good-bye and asked, "May we come again?"

Jenna thought there was just a little more life in the young woman's face than when she'd first come, but she worried about her frailness. "Oh, please do, and I'll walk up to see you, too."

When Simon telephoned later that night, Jenna told him excitedly, "The little red-haired girl and her mother came to tea today. Mrs. Adams watched me clean and wax the candle stands."

"Good—your social life's picking up."

She could picture how he looked as he said that, the smile starting at one corner of his mouth, the dark eyes laughing. *Dear Simon.* "There's a mystery about her."

"Don't push," he cautioned. "Don't ask questions. Let her tell you if and when she wants to. Jenna, just be your natural friendly self. She could use a friend."

"You know something, don't you?" She was intrigued now.

"In her own good time, Jenna. That's important, understand?"

He told her then about some of the things he'd been doing. "I had dinner with the Hamiltons this evening," he said. They had had a pleasant time. He had phoned the apartment a day or two ago too, and talked to both Blake and Daphne. "I told them you'd be having another checkup in about a week and that the physicians were pleased with your progress so far."

"You'll be up? When I go in to Dr. Nicolet again?" she asked, holding her breath.

"I'll be there," he answered in his warm voice. "It sounds as if you're missing me."

She tried to be sensible. "We both are—Goldfisch *and* me."

His voice shook with laughter. "Faulty grammar but a lovely thought, hyacinth-girl."

He said good night, and she put down the telephone

131

and walked dreamily out on the redwood deck to see the stars shining in the night sky dark blue above her. She felt happy and content and alive again—and cherished. Because Simon had called . . .

Because Simon had called? She sank down on the bench with a little thud. Good heavens! When on earth had she fallen in love with Simon?

Chapter 8

The days of lovely summer weather began to form their own small pattern now. There were brisk morning walks with the Lab to see her friends at Echo, visits with Megan Adams, and times when Beth came to play. There were restful hours with Scott's *Waverley* and *Rob Roy* and her own favorites, *Ivanhoe* and *Quentin Durward*, and brief naps in the sunshine on the pier or wherever she chose to place her head. Each day she spent happy hours of work on the furniture project.

She ate simple meals—meat, cottage cheese and honey, plenty of fresh vegetables and fruit. Her skin glowed with health. She was sleeping well at night too, going early to bed and waking before six in the morning to let out the dog and then watch the pale golden colors of sunrise touch Little Bay Lake.

Each week she wrote a long letter to Martha Hamilton and either enclosed a message to be forwarded to her sister and brother or requested Martha herself to telephone them with news of her improvement.

There was no doubt in Jenna's mind that she was almost back to normal, perhaps already in even better health than just before the accident, but Dr. Nicolet insisted that she must have another five or six weeks of quiet living, and then they'd arrange a thorough final examination.

She kept busy, for when she wasn't busy she thought too much—and it was always of Simon.

He had been up two times since that night in mid-June when Jenna had looked up at the stars and acknowledged to herself how much she loved the tall, dark-haired physician with the Irish grin and the intelligent brown eyes. Simon had arrived late in June to take her to Minowac for that appointment with the doctor, and then came again for four vacation days over the Fourth of July.

They had a glorious time. The first day Jenna packed a picnic lunch and Simon took her swimming at the cove. They drove over in the Porsche, with Goldfisch along too, and they sunned themselves on the sandy margin of the little bay, and swam in the cool, blue water, their laughter blending with summer sunshine and the call of birds.

When they were hungry, Jenna spread a clean, white luncheon cloth, one she had found at the cottage, and began to set out the food.

Simon came over to look down at the tablecloth, which was neatly cross-stitched in faded shades of blue. "My mother made that long ago when she was about ten, I think it was," he said, drying off his arms and sandy legs with a huge towel. He bent down and picked up one corner of the cloth. "Here's her name and the date, worked right into the design: Anne Davida Stafford, age ten, 1917."

He put his arm around her shoulders as she put down ham sandwiches and fried chicken and drew her close. "She would have liked you, Jenna," he said.

His embrace was casual and presently he let her go, and she finished setting out peaches and sweet cher-

133

ries, pickles, lemonade, and the brownies she had baked, while he lounged in the grass whistling softly and watching her with a thoughtful expression in his dark eyes.

They had come to the cove once more, bringing Beth to swim, and the memory of Beth's crows of happy laughter as the little girl rode on Simon's shoulders in the water still gave Jenna a thrill. The child had not spoken, of course, but Jenna was getting used to that and asked no questions, neither of Megan nor Simon.

Jenna had an appointment with Dr. Nicolet on the morning following the holiday. Simon packed his bag the night before and stowed it in the front of the Porsche. "I'll be leaving right from town," he said when he saw the questioning look on her face. "Megan Adams is going to give you a ride back."

She didn't say anything, and Simon shrugged and went into her bedroom to use the telephone. He had made quite a number of long-distance calls this time, she thought, not with curiosity but with a kind of sadness that there was so much of Simon's life about which she knew nothing.

The telephone rang at midnight and a sleepy Jenna picked it up and heard the operator say, "Ready on your call to California, Dr. Fraser." She grabbed up her old robe and waited in the living room, half asleep, until he came out again.

"Sulking, Miss Jennifer Anne?"

She shivered and he caught up her hands. "You're freezing. Maybe this will warm you," he said and kissed her hard.

"Jenna . . . hyacinth-girl." He spoke softly, and it was as if star shine and sunlight mingled in his voice when he said her name.

134

"See you in the morning," she said fiercely. "Good night again."

In the morning it was July fifth and Simon's vacation was over.

On the way back to Little Bay in her big Lincoln, Megan Adams saw the tears gathered in Jenna's eyes and asked, "Did you get bad news?"

It had been good news, in fact. Four more weeks, the physician had said, and she'd be out of the woods. Jenna had laughed with him and Simon at his little joke, but her spirits were cellar-level because she didn't want to leave the cottage—not in four weeks, not ever. And she had hated to say good-bye to Simon today.

"No. Good news, actually. I'm just not fond of farewells."

Megan sighed. "Who is?"

She and Beth stayed for lunch, eating leftovers at the kitchen table with Jenna. "When did you get so interested in antique furniture?" Megan asked, her eyes on the newspapers spread out under the sideboard and the table in the living room.

"I've always been, as long as I can remember. Each is a piece of living history to me." Jenna pointed to the Hepplewhite table. "That table of Simon's has three insertable extension leaves, Megan. Fully extended it can seat fourteen—with little fuss. But tables like that didn't even exist until the 1800s. Up to that time, small tables had to be grouped together, as many as were needed, to seat the people for every blessed meal."

Megan groaned. "Heaven help the poor housewife with a large family. I suppose they ate in shifts many times."

135

"Well, certainly the families with only one table had to do just that," laughed Jenna.

Megan watched her take an old, well-washed man's linen handkerchief, fold it into a small square, and place a thick dollop of paste wax on the inside. Then she rubbed over the table's surface in a continuous circular motion with just the right amount of pressure on the folded cloth.

Jenna explained, "You must keep the wax-pad moving like this all the time so that the solvent—that's the turpentine—evaporates and leaves behind the thinnest deposit of hard wax."

Megan tried it next and Beth came near, watching with interest while her mother worked on the top of the table.

That day in early July marked the start of many similar sessions with the two of them washing, then waxing and polishing shield-back chairs, a Pembroke table, the cherrywood highboy, the sofa table, and the Queen Anne tea table. Everything in the living room shone with a first coat of wax polish. Jenna was rather proud of the way things had begun to look.

Inevitably a day arrived when Megan, resting on the redwood deck while Jenna knit, looked down at the lake shore where Beth romped with Goldfisch and said, quite simply, "You're a good friend, Jenna. You've never asked—not once, not a single question—but you must have wondered about me."

With quick intuition of what was coming, Jenna warned, "Don't tell me anything at all unless that's what you really want to do."

Megan looked at her doubtfully. "I don't want to burden you, Jenna, but it's time you knew about us."

She craned her head a bit to check on Beth, who was lying on her stomach on the pier and watching minnows chase each other in the clear lake water. The Lab was close at her side.

"My husband's dead, Jenna. He was a physician, killed in an automobile accident in early April along with our eight-year-old twin sons." She had gone quite white, but she made no attempt to evade Jenna's shocked gaze.

"It was one of those terribly tragic things, Jenna. There had been a bank robbery in Madison, and several police cars were chasing them at high speed on the expressway. The robbers shot back at the nearest squad car; a stray bullet struck one of my husband's tires and his car went out of control and over the embankment. Beth survived. Completely unhurt. She'd been asleep in the back, they think, but both boys and Jason perished in the crash. I was at home."

"Oh, Megan," breathed Jenna, "how does a woman endure such grief?"

Immeasurable sorrow was in the soft hazel eyes. "One endures. There was still Beth . . . and the new baby. Jason and I hadn't planned to have another child. I'm thirty-five and he was forty, and three children seemed enough. But now I'm glad—so glad. Perhaps it will be a little boy. That would ease the torment of memory a little, Jenna. A girl would be nice, too. But boy or girl, I desperately want this new child of Jason's. Beth and I and the baby will be a family, almost."

Jenna sighed. No wonder Simon had cautioned her! "I can't tell you how proud I am to know you, Megan Adams. You're a wonderful, brave woman."

Megan disagreed at once. "No, not very brave at all. I ran away, Jenna, just as soon as the roads opened up here. Away from all the splendid friends and neighbors and relatives and their very real sympathy, and

137

away from all the do-gooders too, who insisted that I must never be left alone.

"Dear God, I just *had* to be alone awhile . . . can you understand that? To lick my wounds, to face the nights of loneliness and the days of grief, to remember—and to begin to forget—"

In the kitchen the teakettle whistled, and Jenna made tea and brought the two cups out on the deck, with milk and cookies for Beth. "Yes, I think I can understand that. And part of it was for Beth too, wasn't it?" Jenna asked quietly.

Megan folded her hands together, tightly. "Since the accident she's spoken very little. You've noticed that, of course. Once in a while a word or two to me. It's from shock, the psychiatrists tell me. Nothing permanently wrong. A child who becomes hysterically mute from one shock either recovers dramatically following another or, in time, with plenty of love and a chance to regain confidence in her world, usually improves gradually."

Jenna said, "And to think I thought *I* had troubles." She leaned over the railing and called to Beth, and both women watched the child look up at them and wave, then pat the Lab and come running to join them.

"You wait and see, Megan dear . . . before this summer's over that small redhead is going to wake up one day and talk our arms off!"

Megan finished her tea. "She was such a jabber-box—"

Jenna went to the steps to meet Beth and show her the milk and cookies. The little girl hugged her and gave her mother a wide, happy smile.

"Will you go back to Madison for the baby's birth?"

"Oh yes," Megan replied. "I'm just a partial runaway. I've promised both my obstetrician there and

138

Jason's sister Betsy that I'll return by August twenty-fifth. That's easily a month before term. Meanwhile, kind old Dr. Nicolet is my temporary primary-care physician, counsulting with my Madison OB man after each of my checkups.

"It's so peaceful up here, Jenna. I'll hate to leave. Jason and I loved the lodge . . . and the boys adored it." Megan bit her lip, hard. "I'll always keep it, Jenna. Someday I'll be happy again—at least, everyone tells me that. But meanwhile, it's been a lovely place of refuge. I've found myself again."

She smiled at Jenna and stood up then, saying, "Come on, young one—time to go home."

Jenna stood in the clearing, waving until Beth and her mother had disappeared from her view, and then she went into the house and waxed furniture vigorously until she was so weary that she knew she'd sleep.

She couldn't imagine her world without Simon. She missed him tonight rather dreadfully. "And a lot of good that does you, my girl," she admonished herself.

Early next morning she walked briskly down the road to the Echo general store. Goldfisch trotted along at her side.

"You've seen the headline in the Chicago paper?" Linda queried with raised eyebrows.

"No." Jenna felt uneasy as she picked up the newspaper.

"She did it," Linda said softly. "She said she would, you know. If he didn't dance to her tune."

It was on page one. Appalled, Jenna read: CHICAGO HEIRESS WEDS IN L.A. (More Pictures, Page 3) . "Why, he's *old!*"

"Fifty-two—not old, Jenna. Just old compared with Simon," Olav said gravely.

Simon—Jenna stared at the pictures until they were confused and meaningless, and she was seeing only Simon's thick, dark hair and warm, intelligent eyes. The news story said that it was the third marriage for the California senator, the first for the department-store heiress . . . the bride had been radiant in white silk . . . the couple was honeymooning in the Greek Isles, guests of a multimillionaire yachtsman.

Jenna refolded the paper and placed it back on the counter.

"He's well rid of her." Linda was blunt. "Only, I hope it doesn't break his heart."

It was Friday, and Jenna had an appointment with Dr. Nicolet on the next Tuesday. There was a good chance Simon might be on his way north.

"How do you make a cherry pie?" she asked Linda, and Olav laughed, following her thoughts, and walked slowly back to their own rooms to get a cookbook for her.

But Saturday and Sunday passed without Simon. Megan and Beth helped to eat the pie. Jenna worried all weekend until she finally found the courage to telephone his apartment.

Nothing . . .

She dialed his office, the hospital, and then his home again. Dr. Fraser could not be located.

Monday night she cried herself to sleep, emotionally too exhausted to do anything except weep. The sound of a key in the lock and the Lab's sudden bark awakened her just before three o'clock. She reached for the switch of her bedroom lamp.

"Hello, Jenna," Simon said. There were lines on his face that had not been there one month ago. He put out an unsteady hand and touched the scar on her cheek.

For a second she froze. Time skidded by. . . . She could have stepped aside or pushed him away; instead, she went into his arms and kissed him, thankfully, joyously. "I'm so terribly glad to see you. Simon, I've been worried. Where have you been? I called and called the apartment."

He was shaking, shaking to pieces with cold and unhappiness, and he had been drinking—she could smell brandy on his breath. She reached out and pulled off his jacket, flung it over the chair. He seemed to relax a little then, and she pushed him down on her bed and knelt to untie his shoes.

She could taste salt in her mouth and she realized she was crying. Weeping for Simon . . . "You're exhausted," she said, and gently stroked the hair back from his forehead.

The dark eyes opened. "Half dead." His voice was harsh with weariness. "I wanted to talk to you, Jenna."

Her throat ached with tears. "I know . . . please sleep, Simon. We'll talk in the morning."

"Come here," he begged, pulling her down to lie beside him.

She held him close in her arms, cradling his dark head against her breast, feeling a bittersweet joy that he had come to her for comfort. Her heart swelled with emotion.

He was asleep so soon. Within seconds. She lifted the blankets and gently covered him.

"Sleep," she murmured softly. "Go to sleep, my darling."

Lightly, she kissed his brow, his quiet mouth, the large, capable hands. Blinded then by a haze of tears, she wrapped a woolen blanket around herself and sank down in the slipper chair to watch beside him.

When the sky lost its darkness and an early dawn wind moved through the pine trees, she went quietly to Simon's empty room to sleep awhile.

* * *

She drifted awake through layers of dreams, with the Lab's head resting heavily on her arm and Simon leaning in the doorway watching her with haunted eyes. Memory flooded back and she pulled her robe close about her throat. "Are you all right now, Simon?"

He came to her and sat on the edge of the bed, seizing her hands. "God, Jenna, what did I do to you?" He said stiffly, asking her because he had to know, "I can't remember . . . I've wakened in your bed . . . Jenna, did I—?"

She came completely awake then, knowing what he was asking but able at first to only stammer, "I—you—" in a completely disoriented way.

His eyes searched her face for the truth and she told him. "You never touched me, Simon. You were exhausted, half dead with fatigue, and you collapsed on my bed. I took off your jacket and shoes, covered you up, and slept in here."

His intelligent eyes narrowed slightly. "I seem to be quite thoroughly undressed beneath this robe."

"You must have awakened later then, either uncomfortable in your clothes or perhaps too warm under the covers." She said, hesitantly, "Simon, don't *worry* so—"

He lifted her hands to his lips and smiled at her in a shattering way. His voice unsteady, he told her, "I've led no monk's life, Jenna. It was killing me to think I might have harmed you. Not you, Jenna. God, *not you*—"

She looked away because she could not face the anguish in his eyes.

"I know about Patrice," she said shakily. "I understand how you feel."

A strange expression crossed his face. He said, "I wonder if you do, my little innocent."

* * *

Simon stayed only long enough to take her into Minowac to see Dr. Nicolet.

"You're coming back again soon?" she asked hopefully.

He was vague about that. There was a conference in London next week which he planned to attend . . . an invitation to Maine. He would see, he promised.

She looked a little wistful. "I'll take care of Goldfisch for you," she said, "but soon I have to be thinking of going home."

He said curtly, "Not yet, you won't," and kissed her good-bye. All of it was so unlike Simon that she cried when she told Linda. "I don't understand men at all!"

In sympathy Linda said, "Dear, they find us a bit difficult too."

The August days passed in summer glory. There were sweet-smelling wild berries in the clearing by the wash-house now. Blue gentians, stately Queen Anne's lace, and goldenrod replaced the iris and sky-blue columbine and the wild roses.

Jenna saw the first pale tinge of scarlet on the sumac and promised herself she'd stay only until Megan left for Madison with Beth.

Simon had not been back for almost four weeks. Oh, he had telephoned every six or seven days—and once all the way from England. Her heart had beat fast when she heard his voice. But it was Simon she was missing and would for the rest of her life.

Chapter 9

All night a storm had threatened. Lightning sliced through the sky, and thunder growled and roared around the lake like a struggling, wounded animal. The atmosphere was heavy, but no rain fell.

Toward dawn a brisk breeze began to blow. Jenna sat up in bed, listening. It was difficult to sleep, for the wind made the cottage full of unusual noises. Goldfisch, too, was uneasy.

If only it would rain!

By morning the storm itself seemed to have passed their area, but the sky remained an uncertain gray-blue color. Although it was Sunday, Jenna decided that she had better finish the laundry before it rained again. She pushed the wire laundry cart along the path to the shed, sitting out on the grass writing letters and reading while the washer and dryer operated. She soon found herself daydreaming, wishing Simon would come again.

The Lab had loped off into the woods when the clothes were ready, so she returned alone to put away clean towels and sheets and her own fresh clothing.

While they had been gone, the wind had changed. It seemed to be coming from the south now, blowing rather fiercely in her face as Jenna ran down to the pier. White caps rode each wave. She stood watching the lake until the first raindrops splattered down. When Goldfisch bounded back to the cottage only ten minutes later, it was raining so heavily that it took several towels to rub him dry.

Just before lunchtime Jenna telephoned Echo. "I

don't suppose the Kittelsens are back from Duluth yet, are they, Benny?"

"They're staying over another two days—back on Tuesday," came the cheerful reply.

Jenna chewed her lip. "Benny, what's up? Isn't this wind rather strong for just an ordinary storm? We're too far north for tornado country, aren't we?"

Benny said he didn't know; he'd never seen a twister. They'd get weather warnings on the radio if there was danger, he said. "If you're nervous, Miss Wilson, why don't you come over here?"

She observed, "It's probably one of those summer storms Dr. Fraser said they sometimes get in August. Electricity knocker-outers."

Benny asked her if she needed candles.

She had candles—Simon had seen to that. Jenna went from room to room, placing them in their neat glass chimneys, with packets of safety matches alongside each one. Just in case . . .

She prowled about the house, feeling restless. Finally, she got out the wax to apply the third coat to the satinwood desk in the living room, for the second coat was properly hard now and would not dissolve in the volatile solvent while she worked. She applied the paste wax generously, rubbing it into the surface of the desk with the wax-soaked cloth, working constantly in a circular motion and with the same amount of pressure.

At intervals Jenna stepped back from the desk to rest her hands and admire the shine that was building up. Before she returned to Chicago, she thought there'd be time to apply a fourth coat of wax, and the hard, durable surface that would be built up then would surely protect the lovely little desk until—

Jenna dropped down on the floor and contemplated

145

the honeysuckle carvings of the forward-facing legs. *Until when?*

She made herself stop and go to the kitchen and fix a cup of soup for lunch. She sat at the kitchen table and chewed carrot sticks and a stalk of celery while the soup heated. "Face it!" she commanded that other Jenna. " . . . Until Simon marries and his wife takes over the care of the Connecticut antiques."

Would she, whoever she was, polish the sideboard with care and would she notice the careful mend of one reeded leg? Jenna had found it, running her hand over the substituted wood. The repair had been so skillfully done that only a loving hand or an expert eye could detect it.

While she washed the few lunch dishes, Jenna noticed the strange look of the sky. It had taken on almost a yellow-green color. She turned off the electrical unit under the teakettle and went to telephone Megan.

Her voice was casual. "Everything okay up your way?"

Megan said they were fine, but there was a different tone in her voice that concerned Jenna.

"I think perhaps I'll take Dr. Nicolet's advice and leave a bit earlier than I'd planned at first," Megan confided. "Perhaps this Tuesday, if I can get organized in two days. Dr. Nicolet wants me back with my own physician in Madison."

Jenna told her, "I'll come right over and pack for you. Don't you do a thing, hear me? You're feeling all right, aren't you, Megan?"

"Yes, I suppose so—just getting anxious. The last six or seven weeks are the hardest. And this weather doesn't help. Don't come now, Jenna, it's started to pour, and it looks like an all-afternoon rain. I promise

146

I won't do anything but rest today, if you're coming tomorrow to help."

Jenna bit her lip, thinking hard, wishing she knew more about pregnancy. "Megan—look, should you be driving the two hundred miles back to Madison by yourself? I could go along."

Megan explained, "Jason's sister Betsy was flying down on the twenty-fifth to drive back with me, but I think that if I leave two weeks earlier I'll be fine by myself. Betsy will come anytime I ask, if I need her, you know."

"I wish you'd call her now and ask her to come for Tuesday," Jenna said.

"Perhaps I shall. Yes, you're probably right. I'll do that."

Megan rang off, promising to call if she needed anything before Jenna came on Monday to help her pack.

Jenna finished the waxing, took a shower, and lay down to rest. She was eager to continue reading Scott's *Kenilworth*. For several hours, she was enthralled with the story of the brilliant court of Queen Elizabeth I and of her friend Lord Robert Dudley, whose lovely young wife Amy stood so innocently in his way to still greater favor with the queen.

Once Jenna had hoped to visit the magnificent ruins of Kenilworth Castle and, like Walter Scott, let imagination restructure the massive keep, the graceful chapel, and John of Gaunt's Banqueting Hall alive again with the red-headed queen, Sir Walter Ralegh, and the future Earl of Leicester.

Once . . . Jenna was realistic enough to admit that the expenses of her accident had probably removed all hope of her pilgrimage to Sir Walter Scott's country for at least another five years. Too bad, she thought regretfully, but she had learned some years ago to face facts.

It was two thirty now, and Jenna peered out the sliding door of the sun deck. The rain seemed to be over, but the day had turned dreadfully hot and sticky. Thunder rumbled in the distance. She walked to the edge of the decking, a bit frightened at the mass of heavy, low-lying black clouds farther to the southwest.

Suddenly in the far distance a streak of swirling air stretched earthward from the blackest cloud, extending down through the greenish haze in the shape of a long, narrow funnel.

Jenna gasped. A tornado!

Already the tall pines and balsams and white cedars were bending in fresh gusts of wind. Bright flashes of lightning lit the tortured sky.

She dashed back into the bedroom. She was frantically dialing Megan's number when the strange roaring sound began. It filled the air and set her ears to ringing, growing louder and louder and louder.

Everything she had ever heard about tornadoes raced through her mind. But there was no basement— no storm cellar that she knew of— *Then find some heavy furniture and crawl beneath it—and wait and hope and pray.*

And, oh God—Beth and Megan . . .

With its large windows the bedroom was too exposed. It was better in the living room. Jenna pushed the sofa over to cover the open side of the Hepplewhite table, which was near an inside wall. She ducked under the table and lay there, terrified, covering her ears yet still hearing a noise like a thousand demented freight trains roaring past. Goldfisch huddled close to her, trembling.

The roar surged by, splintering branches off trees, felling timber, tearing boards from buildings. Thun-

148

der rolled, more distant now. Jenna lifted her head. "I think we made it."

The Lab crawled from under the table, shook himself, and made for the kitchen door. Jenna followed more slowly. Her legs felt weak and a thin film of perspiration bathed her body. Shock, she told herself, and found a sugar cube, eating it rapidly with a throat still dry with fright.

Outside, the rain had almost ceased. The sky above held a few gray rain-clouds, but there were also patches of innocent blue. The sun was trying to come out.

Jenna stood in the clearing, amazed at the little visible damage. One 60-foot pine was down, roots and all. It had crashed across the drive. The spruces and white cedars had lost branches, and green pine needles were strewn everywhere. Near the lake itself the white birches looked more tattered, but Simon's cottage appeared totally undamaged.

Jenna breathed a tiny prayer of thankfulness and flew back into the house to telephone Megan. No dial tone. She tried again. And once again. The phone was definitely out of order.

There was no electricity either. Power lines were probably down for miles around. Well, that was why she had the candles—

While it was still light, she wanted to get to Megan. She fed the dog, then set about to gather candles, matches, her flashlight, extra dog food, *Kenilworth*, her knitting, and the clothing she would need to stay overnight. She was in the kitchen selecting a few articles of food to bring along when she heard the faint noise at the door.

"Beth!" Jenna bent down and hugged the little girl. "Are you all alone? Where's Mother, honey?"

The child's eyes were huge in a frightened, white

149

face. "Please come to Mama." She reached out a hand and tugged at Jenna's. "Come to Mama."

"Oh, darling—yes!" Jenna caught up her overnight case and her handbag. She called the Lab, locked the door, and hurried after Beth across the littered clearing and down the path to the meadow.

The violent storm had barely touched this area. Jenna realized now that Simon's cottage had been on the remote edge of the windstorm. The tornado itself must have passed in a narrow, twisting band somewhere between Simon's cottage and Minowac.

But *between* them and town meant that the main road might be blocked with hundreds of fallen trees toppled across the roadway like so many matchsticks. Jenna shuddered.

Megan was lying on the sofa when they came. She had dark smudges under her eyes. She began to get to her feet, but Jenna took one look at her white, drawn face and gently forced her flat again.

"What's wrong, Megan? Is it the baby?"

Megan blew Beth a kiss. "Poor little girl . . . I frightened her, going all faint like that. I had to send her for you, Jenna, as soon as the rain was over. Sorry—"

Rain! Jenna gave her a thoughtful look, placing a light afghan over the slender body. "Does your phone work? Have you called Nicolet?"

Oh God, please let her phone work.

"Yes—I called Dr. Nicolet about twenty minutes ago. He said they'd had a twister near town. Your phone was out, he said. He told me I should send Beth to get you as soon as the storm was over. Oh, Jenna, I'm so terribly afraid that these are early labor pains."

"Well, we'll see. Don't worry, I'm here now." Jenna swallowed hard and reached for the phone. Miraculously, the instrument hummed and offered a dial

150

tone. Megan still had electricity, too, she noticed. A tornado was a freaky thing.

With shaky fingers she dialed Dr. Nicolet's office. Early labor? The physician would just have to come to them then.

"Jenna? Thank God, you're there." The relief in the old man's voice when he heard her speak was evident. "Listen carefully, my dear."

If this was really the beginning of labor, Mrs. Adams was in trouble, he told her. The baby was lying in a breech position. Changing such a presentation before birth by manipulation from outside the womb was customarily attempted, but there often were dangers in such switching of the child's position. "This is why I asked her to return home to Madison without further delay."

It sounded bad to Jenna. "I think you'd better come out here right away," she said, dismayed.

The quavery voice strengthened then. "You must not let Mrs. Adams see that you are alarmed," he warned her firmly. "Listen to me: I am giving background information so that you will understand how important your help is right now."

Jenna said flatly, "Please continue."

He told her anxiously that the combination of both premature labor and a possible breech birth placed Megan Adams in the high-risk category. She was going to need specialized help to get her baby safely born. Such a birth was harder on the child, too, and the possibility of a cesarean section would need to be considered, with all that entailed.

Jenna felt goose bumps race up her arms.

Dr. Nicolet was in touch with the high-risk obstetric care unit in Madison. Megan's own physician there had been alerted, also. Within an hour a fully equipped plane would be arriving at their local airport. If all went well, Mrs. Adams would be in the Wisconsin Perinatal Center in Madison by five o'clock.

"Now, my dear," he said, "here comes the hard part for you."

Jenna listened, aghast. "Oh, no. I can't drive. You must come to us. Send an ambulance."

"We can't reach you. Not in time. The main road is out. There's fallen timber down in a dozen places where the brunt of the storm hit in the sparsely populated area between you and Minowac. It can't be cleared in time. And it's time that we're fighting now. The only possible way to the airport is for you to go the back way by the old swamp road. It's in poor condition and the highway people advise me that there are trees down and blocking it in two places, but they already have their road crews at work there with chain saws on a first-priority basis. They're expecting you, and by the time you reach the first roadblock on your end, they'll be there cutting a passage through for you."

She whispered, "I can't—I really can't—I'm afraid to drive."

He hesitated. "There's no other way, Jenna. It might mean two lives."

"I'll try," she told him then in a tight little voice.

"Good girl. Put Mrs. Adams in the back seat on her side. The baby gets more oxygen that way. Cover her well. I believe it's a heavy car and should be able to take the swamp road, but it won't be easy driving. Here are the directions, Jenna. Best to jot them down."

A heavy car? It looked like a monster to Jenna as she assisted Megan into the rear seat and positioned her on her side. She placed a small pillow beneath her head and covered her with a woolen blanket she had snatched off a bed.

"You're going to be just fine," she assured her apprehensive friend in the calmest of voices. "Dr. Nicolet says it may be only false labor, but this baby is too important for us to take any chances. So off we go to the airport, my fair lady, and you'll be in Madison General by four thirty."

Megan managed a half smile. "You've got Betsy's number? And you'll take care of Beth for me, won't you? Betsy will come for her on Tuesday, I'm sure." Another pain struck, and she was silent for a few minutes.

"Jenna, thank you for coming. I knew if you could just get to me, everything would be all right. The first pain caught me so unawares, but I'd been feeling a little strange all day. Rather fainty. Is Beth there with you?"

"She's here. She's my sweetie, aren't you, honey?" She popped Beth into the passenger seat, tossed in extra sweaters and clean towels, ran back to the lodge for her purse and spoke to the Lab. "You're in charge, Goldfisch. *Stay*."

For just a second she stood still, staring at the large car, certain she would never be able to drive it. Cold sweat rolled down her spine. Despite all her efforts to remain calm, her hands shook.

She grasped the key and turned on the ignition. Power steering . . . oh, lord, then there'd be power brakes, too. She thought fleetingly of the old blue VW and reversed jerkily down the drive.

They traveled the dirt road at a crawling pace, detouring around puddles and broken branches while Jenna got the feel of the car. Through the open windows came the fresh green smell of crushed pine needles.

Once on the gravel they made better time, and Jenna kept an eye on the mileage. There should soon be a small dirt road leading off to the left. Her sweaty hands slipped on the wheel and she wiped them, one at a time, on her good beige slacks.

She slowed down and glanced at the back seat. Megan lay motionless, her eyes closed.

On Jenna's left appeared a trail, a track just wide enough for one car. Heaven help us if it's like that all the way, she thought, and swung the Lincoln off the gravel road. The swamp road straggled ahead like a shabby, winding ribbon.

They were out of the forest and running alongside the swamp now, sliding in and out of potholes and plowing through mud. Megan groaned once and tried to turn over, and Beth began to whimper.

"I'm sorry—sorry, Megan. I know it's rough," Jenna said. "Stay on your side, please. I think we're halfway there." Which was a lie, of course. But it sounded encouraging, even to Jenna.

In the distance she saw the sheen of water. An alarmingly wide expanse of water right in the road. She watched it with growing apprehension as they approached. "I wonder how deep that is," she said to Beth, bringing the car to a stop.

She got out and surveyed their situation. There was mud ahead, and then a stretch of water about eight feet wide before the little trail climbed out again and meandered on. Could a large car go through that much water? There was swamp on both sides here, so the little trail was the only way. Jenna frowned. She'd better find out first how deep the water was.

She staggered in and waded across, struggling because of the mud that sucked at her loafers. The water came to her knees.

In the swampy ground behind them were the re-

154

mains of several old birch trees. Jenna grasped decaying branches and tore them loose. She placed them lengthwise across the submerged roadway. Where the mud seemed the deepest, she thrust in two branches, upright, to serve her as markers.

Back at the car, Megan was trying to sit up. "What's wrong? Why are we out here?"

"The main road's blocked, Megan. Lie down again—no, on your side. Everything's fine . . . we're nearly there."

Were you supposed to take a car through something like this at high speed—or was it low gear? Jenna wasn't sure, but at high speed Megan could too easily be jarred and hurt, and what good would it all do then? She packed sweaters around Megan to cushion her from bumps and checked Beth's seat belt.

Placing her hands firmly on the wheel, she set the car in motion. Terrified, she thought of Simon, and said his name to herself, over and over. *Simon. Simon. Simon.*

The car lurched through the water and rolled to a dead stop. One wheel was off the trail and sinking into the softer surface of the mud. Jenna restarted the motor and with a burst of speed felt the car pull out and settle back on the track. She spun the wheel and the Lincoln surged ahead.

"You're all dirty," Beth said in mild surprise.

"Oh, baby," Megan wept softly, "you're talking to Jenna. Oh, bless you both—my little girl—"

Beth lifted startled eyes. "You lost your shoe, Jenna."

Jenna looked down for an instant. Mud to her knees—no left shoe—blood on her hands— "That's the style for today, sweetie," she laughed.

They negotiated the last of the swamp section and the track turned south again into the woods toward

Minowac. The important thing now was to make the best time possible. Safely possible.

She stole a quick look at the mileage. They had come eight miles. Five more to go.

"Jenna?" Megan's voice was strained.

She braked gently and shot out of the car to bend anxiously over the woman in the rear seat. Megan opened anguished eyes. "Jenna—a towel? I think—"

Jenna heard her voice saying comforting things, phrases that came to her out of nowhere. She thrust two clean towels gently beneath Megan—wincing at the sight of blood—pulling them up between her knees, covering her carefully again with the blanket. She placed a sweater rolled up beneath her to elevate the hips . . .

"You're doing fine, just fine," she crooned. "We're almost there, Megan. Just a little farther." The Lincoln moved on at a snail's pace until the road firmed again beneath their tires.

"Listen," Jenna said to Beth, "do you hear something?"

They were deep in the woods now, moving along at a faster rate.

Beth tilted her small red head. "I hear a noise."

"So do I! Oh, Beth, sweetie, it's the road crew!" She looked back at Megan. "We're *really* almost there now, Megan."

Men with chain saws were ripping through the trunks of uprooted trees, clearing the road. When the Lincoln came in sight, the men all stopped working and stood up and cheered.

"Why?" asked Beth.

"Oh, darling—they're so glad to see us," Jenna said, with tears smarting her eyes. She slowed the car, guiding it gently through the narrow passages. The foreman cupped his hands and shouted to her, "Three miles—dead ahead."

She waved and called her thanks, then settled down to drive. She felt as if she had been driving forever.

Ahead, they saw a faint light. A man was waiting for them, lifting a lantern high, waving them on. She drove through an open gate, across a grassy field, and stopped in front of a metal shed that had small airplanes tied down on one side of it.

She was fumbling with the door latch when the car door opened. She heard Dr. Nicolet say "Thank God," and she stumbled out.

From then on, things moved swiftly. There were people eager to help. A stretcher-bed was ready for Megan aboard the specially equipped blue-and-silver Beechcraft Baron 58 that had arrived from Madison.

The Baron's team included a pilot and a young obstetrician-fetologist and a plump, smiling perinatal nurse. Jenna took one look at them—clean, shining, specialized, confident, competent—and sought out the nurse. The woman's smile faded a little when she saw her bleeding hands and muddy legs. Jenna explained worriedly about the towels and the nurse assured her, "There's oxygen aboard, blood, plasma—whatever she'll need. And her baby's heartbeat will be monitored all the way. We'll see to everything, my dear. You've certainly done your part."

Jenna stopped by the stretcher. Megan asked again, "You'll take care of Beth?"

She promised, "You know I will." Beth leaned over and kissed her mother and put her hand in Jenna's. "Don't worry, Mama. I'll stay with Jenna and Simon until you feel better."

Jenna said, in a whisper, "God bless—see you soon, Megan."

They watched the Baron turn and taxi down the

157

runway. They saw liftoff and watched silently until the Beechcraft was just a Madison-bound speck in a summer sky.

Reaction set in. Jenna sank down on the grass and pulled off her remaining shoe. "I can't stand up anymore," she apologized to Dr. Nicolet, who now was regarding her with concern. "How many hours did we take to get here?"

"Not quite forty minutes. You're soaked, child. Wet right through. Put this sweater around your shoulders and let's look into getting some dry clothes for you."

Forty minutes! "It seemed like several lifetimes," she admitted.

"Here comes another plane," a mechanic sang out.

A red-and-white Cessna turbo-310 circled the small field and headed in.

"That would be Simon," John Nicolet guessed. A smile spread across his face.

Jenna was too weary to move. She watched the chartered Cessna land, turn, and taxi toward the shed. Then the plane's door opened and a tall, dark-haired man stepped out on the wing, said something to the pilot, and swung himself to the ground.

Jenna was on her feet and running.

With long strides, Simon started toward them. Halfway, he saw the girl and stopped. He put down his black bag and held out his arms, and Jenna ran into them and buried her head against his chest. She leaned against him, laughing, crying a little, and he kissed her wind-tangled hair and her mud-streaked forehead, and then her lips. They clung together.

And then Simon said, "Jenna—Jenna—let me look at you, darling."

He put his hands on her arms and gently turned her to face him. "You're safe," he said wonderingly. "I've been out of my mind with worry about you. First the

158

report of a tornado—then the phone was out—and no one with any news of you."

"I'm safe—only a little the worse for wear."

His smile faded for he was looking at her now, *really* looking, and he saw the blood on her hands, and her bare feet, and her mud-caked legs, and felt her sweat-soaked blouse.

"I'm all right, Simon," she told him quickly, for she saw the stricken look in his eyes.

He said, "My God, Jenna, you're dirty."

He scooped her up in his arms and carried her into the metal shed where he stripped off her wet blouse and slacks and rubbed her all over with a towel, hard, until her skin glowed pink. Then he rolled her up in a blanket, sat her in a chair, and poured hot coffee from the mechanics' percolator down her throat.

And all the while John Nicolet sat there, smiling calmly, and telling Simon all that had happened.

"No wonder I couldn't reach you," Simon said slowly. All the laughter faded from his eyes and he came and knelt beside her and kissed her mouth, and gently examined her poor, scratched hands.

"From the birch branches," she explained. "I put them in the pothole to keep the car from sinking in the mud."

He cleaned the small wounds, bandaged one palm. She was quite unprepared for the tenderness in his eyes and in his arms as he reached to enfold her.

"Hello, Simon," said an interested little voice. "Are you kissing Jenna?"

"Well, well, well," Simon drawled, swinging around to look at Beth, who had come in with the mechanic and was now seated happily on John Nicolet's knee. "Something new has been added, I can hear."

He turned back to Jenna, whose face was flushed

with happiness, and raised his eyebrow inquiringly. "When?"

"Just this afternoon."

It was time to start for home. Simon brought her to her feet, and with one arm around her shoulders and one of his hands holding Beth's, he led them to the Lincoln.

The main road, of course, was still blocked and the only route back to the cottage was by the swamp road. The highway crew had finished their work and were packing up their tools as the Lincoln arrived. Jenna, still wrapped in the scratchy blanket, waved to the men. She saw Simon put something in the foreman's hand and say, "Tonight the beer's on me," and the men cheered and whistled while they drove down the trail and out of sight.

When they came to the wide pothole, Simon stopped and walked over to the water. He looked at it for a long moment and then he came back, tight-lipped, to the car and put his arms around her, saying nothing, just holding her.

She had taken a quick look at the birch branches she had fixed earlier and the old terror came flooding back, but with Simon's arms holding her crushingly close she felt protected . . . safe.

"My sweet girl—my brave girl," Simon said. The deep voice was husky and unsteady.

He put Beth flat in the back seat and told Jenna to close her eyes. She would have done that anyway, completely confident in Simon and whatever he did. She felt the thrust of speed, a jarring sensation, and they were safely over. "We'll not trust our luck there a third time," Simon muttered grimly, and she could see the tension leave his face. "John says the main road will be clear by tomorrow noon."

They drove up to the lodge first to pick up the

faithful Goldfisch and some clothes for the little girl. Jenna went in and telephoned Beth's Aunt Betsy in Madison and told her of the day's happenings.

"Ask her if she can come for Beth tomorrow, on Monday," Simon asked in a low voice. Jenna arranged that too, and then Betsy Adams promised to relay news about Megan to them if they'd call back later that same evening.

Simon's cottage was waiting for them, the kitchen windows shining a sunset-gold-and-pink welcome as the Lincoln rolled to a stop. Simon got out and looked around at the fallen pine tree and branches, and came to her, putting his hands on either side of her face and looking deep into her eyes. "I've been given a second chance at happiness," he said humbly. "Have I told you that I love you?"

She shook her head, because he hadn't yet and she had wondered.

"I love you, darling," he told her very quietly and she blinked back the tears that suddenly blinded her green eyes and smiled at him.

"Me?" she whispered.

"You." He tucked in the folds of the blanket and muttered something that Jenna did not hear, and then he carried her into the house.

"Welcome home, love," Simon said.

Beth watched them both with a little frown. "I'm awful hungry," she volunteered, "and I didn't have any lunch."

Simon swung the child high in the air. "Neither did I, Beth," he teased her. "Clean up and get dressed," he told Jenna. "You're lucky we have a visitor."

She saw the look on his face when he said that, and her heart began a rapid pounding that tinged her cheeks with pink. She went quickly into her room and found what she needed for a shower.

The bath water was cold, the electric stove didn't work, and there were no lights, but Simon located his old Primus and warmed a can of beans and franks and cooked coffee for them. Jenna made a salad, sliced tomatoes, and found three chocolate bars, and the three of them ate by candlelight at the beautifully waxed Hepplewhite table.

While Jenna bathed Beth and helped her get ready for bed, Simon drove back to the Adams's lodge to telephone Madison.

Jenna, with the Lab at her side, was waiting in the clearing for him when the big car returned to slide quietly into a parking place beneath overhanging balsam branches. Above them a full moon gleamed, and Jenna could hear the haunting night call of owls. Goldfisch whined and bounded off to the Lincoln.

Simon came to her and looked down at the white oval of her face. "A boy," he said. "C-section, but all's well with them both. Young Jason's not quite five pounds. He's in their Newborn Intensive-Care Unit, but they're anticipating no real problems. He's eager to live, her doctor told me. He also said Megan is very happy. I called the hospital myself after I'd talked with Beth's aunt."

Jenna's throat grew thick with tears. It was all too much for mere words.

"Wisconsin's got quite a setup." There was admiration in Simon's voice. "Megan is one of theirs, you know, the widow of a highly respected, popular physician, but they functioned for her the same as they would have done for any pregnant woman needing them . . . with everything they've got."

Jenna said uncertainly, "Dr. Nicolet mentioned a specially equipped and staffed perinatal center in Madison. I suppose that's where Megan went. But why

162

so far, Simon? Surely there are places closer than the state capital."

"What a moon!" Simon pulled her down to sit beside him on the step. "A good many, darling. Fine places, well equipped with splendid staffs and all the modern electronic equipment to help babies get safely born. Centers like these operate vans and ambulances specially equipped to roll to the rescue when they have to go out and bring in a high-risk pregnant woman or a newborn already in trouble. However, when distance is too great—like in Alaska—or if floods, hurricanes, or tornadoes block the roads for a center's ambulance, they fall back on other means. There are NICUs all around this nation, and that stands for Newborn Intensive-Care Units, remember, that bring in their patients by helicopter or airplanes furnished with highly trained teams and prewarmed incubators.

"They brought in young Jason, of course, in the most natural incubator of all—Megan herself. And so long as she had to go airborne anyway, they took her directly back to her own Regional Center—the one in Madison where her own physician was, too."

Jenna brushed one small tear away. "Jason Adams . . . I'm so glad it was a son, Simon."

"I have some champagne to 'wet the baby's head.' We'd better go in," Simon said. "I suppose Beth is sound asleep?"

She checked first on Beth, fast asleep, curled up in a little ball on one side of Jenna's bed. Then she went to Simon.

He was watching for her by firelight. Goldfisch lay contentedly at his feet. Simon put out an arm and drew her down beside him on the sofa, stroking her hair, kissing her as if he had every right.

"We have to talk," he said, sliding an arm around

163

her waist and pulling her head down against his chest. She could hear his powerful heartbeats, and she lay there quietly against him.

"Tired?" he asked.

She was, but she didn't want to move. Not ever.

He said, "You're going back to Chicago tomorrow. I'll close up the Adams's place in the morning. Beth's aunt is getting a ride here. She figures she'll arrive around noon, and she'll give us a lift into town in the Lincoln. We'll catch the mail plane out at four ten. Olav's keeping the Lab for a week or so until we get back. Everything's arranged."

Jenna pulled away from him, astonished. "Tomorrow?"

He touched the tip of her nose. "With me." He bent his head and his mouth found hers for a heart-stopping moment.

Intense happiness raced through her. Her arms crept up around his neck, and she felt Simon tremble. His arms tightened around her, and then he was kissing her in a different way, deeply, passionately.

Jenna made a small sound and Simon thrust her from him and said unsteadily, "And that's why you're going back to Chicago tomorrow, my sweet."

"I know I'm old-fashioned," she whispered. "Do you mind terribly, Simon?"

"I love you just the way you are, my little innocent." His hand caressed the curve of her cheek. "You'll marry me, Jenna?"

She relaxed against him. "Oh, darling, yes. Yes! Yes! I didn't know—you hadn't asked, you see—"

He silenced her very effectively.

A little later she asked him, "What did you mean when you said that you had a second chance for happiness?"

She hadn't expected, ever, to be second choice for

the man she loved. But if the man was Simon, she would be second best and gladly. Only, she did wonder a bit at the way he had said it.

He looked at her with such emotion on his face that she was shaken. "The phone was out, and they said the twister had touched down northwest of Minowac and—"

She put her hand to his lips. "Don't—no more—I understand."

"But you don't," he said huskily.

Her head against his shoulder, he told her then how he had felt when the news of Patrice's marriage reached him.

"She phoned me from California, Jenna, offering me one more chance, and then, right after their wedding, she telephoned again—and it was all gone. Everything I'd ever felt for her. Her voice meant nothing. *She* meant nothing. It was as if it had been that way for a long time, and it took her marriage to open my eyes to the fact."

Jenna stared incredulously at him.

"It's true," Simon said simply. "I loved her—once. But it was over and had been over for almost three months, only I didn't know it. I didn't know it until I heard her voice that day of the wedding. And what she said was spiteful, and I thought of you and how you helped people and how kind you were and how gentle— And that day seemed endless because I wanted to come to you, right then, and tell you that I had fallen in love with you, hyacinth-girl. But there were patients to see and hospital visits and unexpected surgery—hours and hours before I could reach you, darling.

"And then, on the way up here, I realized that I must not tell you yet how I felt about you. You weren't my patient, but I had brought you here to my

165

home to recover from an illness. I had made myself responsible. It would be taking an unfair advantage of you, I decided. I had to make myself wait until you were completely well again before I could tell you that I loved you. And it hasn't been easy. The miles I've traveled so that I'd stay away from you—"

He caught her to him, covering her face with gentle kisses. "Oh, my dear," he said, "finding you unharmed today was like a second chance at heaven."

She understood then, and his arms were warm and strong around her. They talked of the future and of Simon's hopes to practice there with Nicolet very soon. They planned their wedding, a simple ceremony in Jenna's childhood church.

"This week—Friday, I should think." Simon said urgently, "Not a day longer than we have to legally wait."

Laughter bubbled up in her throat. "I already have the dress," she said, "but I don't suppose it will fit me yet."

"We're not going to wait for you to fit in any dress," Simon said firmly. "Is it the pink one? Go try it on. I know you have it here."

His dark eyes slowly measured the long, lovely length of her, and she colored becomingly. "You may be surprised," he said knowingly.

And she was. Simply astounded . . .

She came out of the bedroom, a tall, slender girl with sun-bleached blonde hair in a dream of a pink dress, walking on bare tiptoes, for she had no heeled sandals. Her green eyes were wide with astonishment.

She came hesitantly to him. "No wonder all my slacks suddenly seemed too big. It fits . . . I don't understand."

"I do," he said, and he told her. She had been ill to begin with, and had had no appetite for days. Then

166

up here at the cottage she had been active, interested in doing things, restoring the polish on the furniture, cleaning the cottage for him—and she had walked, miles and miles, no doubt.

She listened to him and nodded. "And eaten tons of carrot sticks and Linda's good asparagus and delicious ripe tomatoes." She looked shyly at him and said, "And I've been happy. That makes all the difference."

"You'll look like this for our wedding," Simon told her. "Beautiful. The most beautiful girl in God's world."

"And wearing a springtime dress," she laughed.

Simon said he didn't care if it was an autumn, spring, or winter dress. It was a gorgeous dress and he loved it. And he loved her. He kissed her. Once, with restraint. Then he said wryly, "Go to bed before I break all my noble resolutions."

Chapter 10

It was dark before they reached Chicago. The city simmered in late August heat. Simon asked the cab driver to wait and went up to the apartment with Jenna. Everything looked the same to her . . . everything looked different.

Blake and Daphne were both out, and Simon kissed her good night and said, "You look tired, darling. Promise you'll get right to bed and not stay up talking 'till all hours?"

She pushed damp hair back from her forehead. "I wish this week could just telescope in time—fast—and we were already back at the cottage."

His arms closed around her and he rested his cheek

against hers, gently. "God, I love you, darling." He reminded her, "Sweet, your last checkup with Randall is at ten tomorrow. I'll meet you at the hospital afterwards. We'll have lunch, choose your rings, and pay that call to the courthouse."

She said worriedly, "I have to stop in and clean out my desk. Officially resign, too."

"All in good time. Where would you like to have dinner tomorrow night? The Vendôme? No, let's make it my place, Jenna. You can see the furniture, decide what we want to keep. We'll go to the Vendôme Wednesday evening, after we see the minister."

"Simon."

"What is it, darling?"

"Just—Simon. I love your name. I love you. I'm a little afraid all this is too good to be true."

His mouth found hers in a long good night kiss. "It's true. You'll belong to me now." He said, "I'll call you in the morning. When you tell Blake and Daphne, give them my regards."

And that was the problem, of course. Telling Blake and Daphne . . .

Jenna held her happiness close to her heart, saying nothing until so many hours had gone by that it was Wednesday evening, and Simon was due any minute to take her to Evanston.

When she finally shared her news, Blake looked as if he wanted to strike her. "You're completely out of your mind!" he accused Jenna.

Daphne got very excited and babbled on and on about her problems with Don. She had just been waiting for her sister to come home, all well again, and help her solve them, she said.

By the time the doorbell rang, Jenna was shattered. "Please—come in and talk to them," she begged. "They're dreadfully upset."

168

Simon looked at her pale face. "What have they said to make you so white and jittery?"

Blake and Daphne were standing just inside the doorway, listening, and Jenna said shakily, "Blake, Daphne, you know Simon Fraser. We're going to be married."

"On Friday," Simon said firmly.

Daphne giggled. "Day after tomorrow? You said you'd be wearing the Greensleeves dress for a special occasion within three months, but I didn't think you had it in you to land someone like this."

There was a touch of malice in her laughter, and Jenna winced. "Daphne, you're making that all up!"

Blake glowered and said something about hasty marriages, but Simon joked with him and soon had him relaxed, too. Jenna watched them wistfully.

She said, "Simon, a few problems have come up. Could we talk? Please?"

"Help yourselves," Blake said, "or do you need privacy?"

"They've had privacy," Daphne cried out heatedly. "Weeks and weeks of it in the north woods while we slaved through a Chicago summer."

Jenna was determined not to quarrel. "Daphne," she said reasonably, "you know why I went away. To recover. There was nothing underhanded about my staying in Simon's cottage, so I'd appreciate it if you didn't speak of it as if there were."

"Well, you ran out on us," Daphne insisted angrily. "We depended on you, and you knew it."

Blake waved his hand for silence. "Let's have none of that, Daphne. Jenna's a free agent and has every right to lead her own life. That we were counting on her, presuming that blood was thicker than water, is our mistake, not hers."

He shrugged his shoulders dispiritedly. "I'd never,

169

of course, have entered into a contract with Mark Nelson to open an office with him within the year if I hadn't believed you were in favor of it, behind me all the way."

Simon looked at Jenna, who was gripping her hands together anxiously. In a very cool voice he asked, "This contract . . . would there be a copy for us to examine?"

Blake rose, thrusting his hands into his pockets. "A verbal contract . . . word of honor."

"Hm," said Simon, and he looked next at Daphne. "And you, little sister, have you some problems to air as well?"

She was suspicious of his quiet manner. "What business is it of yours?"

"I plan to marry Jenna. Her peace of mind is important to me."

Daphne flushed. "She should have told me. I mean, really explained. I've always charged my things to her before—"

"And gotten away with it." Simon sounded very controlled.

Daphne wet her lips anxiously. "It's impossible to get along on what I make. I'm just starting out. Jenna knows that. She's always helped me; she should have told me things were going to be different, not just suddenly—"

"Stopped supporting you?" Simon asked.

Blake spoke urgently. "I say, Fraser, that's a bit high-handed. Daphne's just a kid, after all."

Simon's eyes were cold as brown ice. "I believe Jenna's been working to help the two of you since she was younger than Daphne is now. It's her turn to live a little."

Blake shrugged. "She picks a poor time, that's all I can say."

A small frown appeared on Simon's forehead. "You'll understand that I find this somewhat puzzling, Blake? I thought that you were fully employed. Is that correct?"

"Get to the point," Blake said curtly.

Simon was unperturbed. "My point is, Blake, how does it happen that you have allowed Jenna to be burdened with all these bills of Daphne's, some of yours, almost all of the household expenses, the rent each month . . . need I go on?"

An angry gleam flashed from Daphne's blue eyes. "What right have you to come here and tell us how to run our lives? It takes three of us to keep this place going—and Jenna knows that. Or do you want me to find a furnished room? Is that what you want, Jenna?"

Jenna was weeping now. "Please, Daphne—"

"Please, Daphne," mimicked Blake. "Well, she's said it for me, too."

Simon lost his patience. "Before we all ride off in all directions, would you tell a somewhat innocent by-stander what sort of bills we're talking about?"

Blake brightened. "I just happen to have—" He abruptly left the room.

"No," said Jenna firmly. "No."

"No what?" queried Daphne.

"Simon is *not* going to pay our bills."

"Hasn't he enough money to help us out?" Daphne asked.

Simon's dark eyes narrowed. "Shall we stick to the subject in hand? I was inquiring about some bills?"

"Brandy?" Like a well-mannered host, Blake offered him a glass. A small sheaf of papers occupied one portion of the silver tray.

"Thank you. Ah—very nice. Very nice, indeed." Blake sampled the brandy, then held the glass up, studying the golden liquid. "A Hine's? Probably the '58?"

Blake grinned at him. "My word, you hit it right on the head. Nothing but the best in brandy, I always say."

Simon riffled through the bills, extracted one, studied it carefully. "Grant's Liquors . . . er, yes, as you say. But why is the bill in your sister's name?"

"Her credit's good, Blake's isn't," Daphne laughed. She came gracefully to her feet and left the room.

Jenna made a motion to follow her. "Please stay," Simon asked and patted the sofa cushion beside him. "I'd like this to be a joint decision, yours and mine, Jenna."

She came to him slowly, with troubled eyes.

"What I propose we consider—consider only, please note, Blake—is my dividing all these—er—obligations of yours into two sections. One representing those expenses Jenna would have assumed, or might have elected to assume had she been home, the second pile being bills which are naturally your own."

Blake hesitated a moment, then nodded.

"Let's see how things seem then." Simon smiled encouragingly at Jenna, who looked quite wan, and began to sort. He scrutinized each bill, and the second pile was soon the larger.

Daphne had come in, quietly, carrying a light fur jacket. She broke the silence in the room, saying resignedly, "I'll return the jacket. It's only fake fur anyway, but the rest are things I need for my trousseau . . . and I've worn some of them already." Her voice trailed away forlornly.

Simon was interested. "Trousseau? Marriage soon then, I suppose? So what was all that talk of living in a furnished room?"

Daphne fluffed her golden curls. "Don and I quarreled, and I'd already bought all those gorgeous clothes. I get a simply fabulous discount from the places where I model, Simon, and I do love a good bargain."

She twisted her beautifully manicured fingers and looked at her sister. "Don and I made up and we're gloriously happy, only he refuses to be serious again until all these bills"—she extended them appealingly to Simon—"are paid."

Simon took them from her. "All these are for clothes?" He was astounded.

"Well, yes. One or two of them are dresses, and there's one suit too, I believe, that needs taking in a bit, but Jenna's so good at that."

He purposely misunderstood. "Fine. Get them, please."

And when Daphne returned, puzzled, with a mulberry wool suit, a jade-green frock, a love of a long, peach silk dinner dress, and a plain, basic black over her arm, Simon nodded to Jenna. "There's the start of your new wardrobe."

Daphne yelped like a wounded puppy. "But they're all from Greensleeves!"

"How nice. I know you're delighted that Jenna will now fit them, with a bit of adjustment, perhaps, but as you say your sister's quite skilled at that."

Daphne tossed her curls and asked sullenly, "You'll pay the bills, then?"

"Now wait a minute," Blake interrupted. "A girl's family is supposed to buy the trousseau. I don't think—"

Simon interposed smoothly, "By girl's family do you mean Jenna? Or had you planned to—?" He raised his expressive dark eyebrows.

"No, no," Blake said hastily. "It's just that—ah—I

thought Jenna would want to see her sister decently outfitted. You understand?"

"Not quite," Simon admitted, placing Daphne's bills to one side and continuing with the sorting of Blake's.

Daphne came to stand behind him, peering over his shoulder. "What's that one? There's no name on it, Blake. It just says 'Personal—four hundred dollars.'"

Blake's face went white and he jammed his hands into his trouser pockets, angrily. "Just what it says. Personal." He watched tight-lipped as Simon added it to the second pile.

Simon put his left arm around Jenna's waist, pulling her closer. He added sums quickly on a slip of paper, checked his figures, and said, "I make one set a total of $479, Blake. You have personal bills of more than nine hundred dollars."

Jenna gasped and Simon leaned over and kissed her cheek. He picked up the larger pile in his capable hands and held the bills out to Blake. "You would not, of course, be expecting your sister to buy your liquor. Not quite the thing at all, I'm afraid. Nor two new suits, Finchley ties, a weekend—er—for two at French Cove, and some personal peccadilloes such as the four-hundred-dollar item."

Blake's face went from white to red. "At least include the September rent," he sneered.

"But of course," Simon agreed pleasantly. "Let me see, that's $679 then. We'll toss in another twenty-one dollars and clear the phone bill too. I make that seven hundred dollars."

Jenna had shrunk into a silent little bundle of unhappiness.

Simon finished his brandy, set down the glass, and said, "Now let's consider Daphne's." Out came the pencil and the bit of paper. He added, frowned, and

174

rechecked the statements, one by one, against the column of figures.

Blake said gruffly, "Well? What does it add up to?"

Simon was concentrating on the tip of his pencil. "Not quite fifteen hundred dollars, I'm afraid."

"I said I'd return the fur," Daphne pointed out.

"About thirteen hundred then."

There was silence all around them. A tense, thick, uncomfortable quiet.

"Could I see you a minute?" Blake asked Jenna. "Privately?"

She started to rise and Simon put out his hand and touched her arm. "Let's keep this all out in the open, darling. Then there'll be no chance of misunderstanding what's been decided."

Her brother's shoulders drooped and the life seemed drained from his face. "This really must be private," he mumbled.

Jenna looked appealingly at Simon and followed Blake from the room. In the privacy of the kitchen she said wearily, "What is it, Blake?"

"I have some debts no one knows about. I've been gambling. They *must* be paid, Jenna." His eyes were frantic. "I've got to get the money."

"How much?"

He hesitated. "A thousand dollars."

She forced his eyes to meet her own. "How much? The truth this time."

Blake winced. "Two thousand would get them off my back."

Jenna sank down on a chair. "How could you? Blake, how could you!"

He was eager to explain. "It was a mistake, I know that now. I got in over my head. I only went there twice, Jenna. But they're pressing for payment and I can't welsh on a debt like that. I have until the first of the month, and then they'll write my boss."

Jenna shuddered. "I have two hundred left in my savings account."

"Would you ask Simon for it?"

She was stunned. "You mean, on top of the seven hundred and Daphne's thirteen hundred? You can't be serious, Blake."

"I'm damn serious." His voice was agitated now. "How would you like to have that hanging over you? If my boss finds out, he'll not keep me in the office. Where would I go then?"

"Surely you're exaggerating. Have you asked these people to let you pay it off in installments—maybe over the period of a year?"

He looked at her pityingly. "You don't ask these men anything. These are the biggies, Jenna. *They* tell you."

Bewildered, she shook her head. "It's going to take me awhile to think this through. Blake, have you talked to Mr. Hamilton? Would he lend you some money—advance it to you, I mean—against my insurance settlement?"

"I tried that first of all. They cleared all your medical bills and replaced your car with that second-hand Dodge Dart. Final settlement won't take place for months yet, and don't expect it to amount to anything even then. Not with old man Hamilton handling it. He won't put the squeeze on."

"Blake! Stop talking like that. I don't want a cent more than I'm entitled to by law. Accidents aren't for making money." She stared blindly at the table, thinking hard.

"You've got to help me. My name will be mud unless you do, Jenna."

He had picked the one weapon that was sharpest of

176

all. *"Your* name?" Jenna said quietly. "My name, too. Daphne's name. Father's name. A respected, honest, decent name always . . . "

Blake shuffled his feet in embarrassment. "No one will know if you just help me. Help me this one time, Jenna."

She had started back to the living room already, and she turned and looked at him. "I'll help . . . because it seems I must. But no one must ever know this shameful thing, Blake."

He was elated. "Simon'll never miss the money."

"I can't ask Simon," she told him dully. "No, don't bother to ask me why. You wouldn't understand."

When she reentered the living room, Simon rose. He smiled encouragingly at her. "Something that should be told me now?" he asked quietly. When she shook her head, he seated himself again and said, "We're all here once more. I'd like to conclude this discussion, for Jenna and I have an appointment in Evanston to arrange with the minister for our marriage on Friday. I have a check here. I've just written it out for two thousand dollars. It is expressly to cover the seven hundred dollars related somewhat to household expenses and the thirteen hundred of Daphne's back bills. Consider it a wedding present from your sister and me."

He looked Blake straight in the eye. "There will be no more. Is that clearly understood?"

Daphne jumped up and kissed him. Blake simply looked at Jenna.

Her voice sounded odd even to her own ears. "Simon—" she faltered.

Simon placed the check carefully on the side table and waited.

"Simon," she began again, "I—I must ask you to let me have another month or two. I—I need more time." She blinked away hot tears.

177

No one spoke for a minute. Simon looked at her very steadily.

She said, "Simon, I'm so sorry . . . please understand—"

"I'm afraid I don't," he said, with no expression at all in his voice. "Perhaps it has something to do with your conversation in the kitchen?"

She held her breath, aching to tell him, but the opportunity passed because Blake was saying, "Perhaps she's remembering some older loyalties, Fraser."

The tears were sliding down her face as she denied it. "I love you, Simon."

He leaned against the doorway and surveyed the three of them. "Jenna knows that I love her, too," he told them. "But there's more to marriage than love alone. There's something called trust, and unless a marriage has that also, its days are numbered."

Daphne was listening, tense with excitement. Blake drummed his fingers on the arm of the chair, impatient now for all this to be over.

Simon said, "I want all three of you to hear this, for I plan to say it only once. Your help to your sister and brother was undoubtedly needed in the beginning, Jenna. But only then. Let me make that crystal clear. It now serves the opposite purpose, creating a deteriorating effect—weakening Blake's ability to stand up like a man, encouraging Daphne to grow up shallow and self-seeking. And it's harming you, too, my darling.

"There's not much point in our going to Evanston tonight, is there? Not when you've asked me for more time." His face had a bleak look.

He asked suddenly, "Jenna, would you get your purse and come away with me right now? Leave your apartment key behind, you'll not need it again. They have the check—"

178

The unhappiness pierced deep inside her. "I can't—oh, Simon, I want to, and I can't . . ."

His smile was cold. "Call me if you change your mind. I'll wait for your call until Friday."

He was gone and she could not believe it.

Blake said lightly, "At least we're two thousand dollars richer."

She reached for the check, wadded it up into a ball, and threw it at the wastebasket.

"Temper, temper," Daphne chided. "Anyway, you got three dresses and one gorgeous suit out of it."

At that, Jenna flung herself down on her bed and her laughter grew so wild that Blake came in and slapped her, hard, on one side of her face. She crumpled into desolate, heartbroken weeping.

By working patiently with a moderately warm iron, it took Blake barely ten minutes to smooth the wrinkles from Simon's check.

Jenna wakened with a throbbing headache. Thursday . . . She closed her eyes. Simon hadn't telephoned.

She heard Daphne's laugh from nearby. Then Blake's voice— She stood up and called to her sister, "Please get me something to wear into town."

Daphne came and looked at her, speculatively. "You've lost weight all right. Try this." Daphne brought out a dark blue cotton with its own smart braid-trimmed bolero. "How about shoes?"

"I've got some here." Her voice sounded dead. Well, she felt dead—

"Look," said Daphne, troubled now. "You'll make it up. People in love always do. Call him, why don't you?" She felt cheap, seeing the lost look in Jenna's eyes.

179

Blake brought her a cup of coffee. "How do you like it? Black?"

She shrugged. It didn't matter. Nothing mattered. "Black's fine, thanks."

"Er—Jenna," Blake said, hesitantly, "about last night . . . "

"Please. I don't want to talk about it." She couldn't bear that. Not now. "Try me again in a week or two."

It wasn't that she thought things would be better in a week or so. Nothing would probably ever be right again. But, please God, perhaps the hurt would be less. *Maybe tomorrow . . .*

"I'll need the car," she told him. "May I have my keys?"

"Let me drive you," he suggested. "You're not used to Chicago traffic yet. Just tell me where you want to go." He was worried about her. She was too quiet, too still.

They parted in front of the tall office building where she had worked. "Shall I wait?" he asked.

She planned to go shopping after she had talked to Mr. Hamilton. "Be here around noon," she said. "Thanks for the ride."

He got out of the car and came around to where she was standing. She was slim now, so chic in the navy outfit, and really beautiful with the scar all covered up like that with makeup. He watched her walk through the doorway, her blonde hair swinging at her shoulders, and wondered why he suddenly felt she was the lovelier of his two sisters.

Parker Hamilton stood up to greet her. "Jenna, my dear, what's gone wrong? Martha and I had so hoped—"

"Please," she begged him, "I'll weep if I have to talk about it. Maybe someday—but not now." She bit her lip, fighting for control. "I resigned on Tuesday. May

I reapply on Thursday? If my job's filled, I'll under-stand. I just wondered . . . "

The old attorney wished she would break down and weep. "Weeping I could handle," he told Martha that evening. "It was the icy control of her emotions that frightened me."

"You gave her back her job, of course?"

"Of course. Glad to have her back. Well—you know what I mean, Martha. Damn it, I like that girl."

"We both do," his wife said thoughtfully. "I would have staked my emeralds that Simon meant to have her. What's gone wrong?"

"I'm not certain," Parker Hamilton said very quietly, "but I have a mighty strong suspicion."

Martha considered this information. As an attor-ney's wife she knew better than to question her hus-band, but she felt free to ask this much, "I think I'd like to talk to Simon. Would you mind?"

"Not at all, my dear. Not at all."

But in Simon's apartment the phone merely rang and rang; and his office answering service related that Dr. Fraser was presently out on calls. Would she leave her number so he could ring back, please?

Jenna came in from shopping. She had bought three dresses to wear to the office and, with the navy outfit she was wearing, that should do nicely. She walked straight to the telephone and dialed Simon's office. Would she leave her number? the service inquired effi-ciently.

She called his apartment, but the phone was not an-swered. Desperately eager to hear his voice, she called Augustana Hospital. She was told that Dr. Fraser's name was not lighted on the board; it was presumed he was not at the hospital.

Jenna made a cup of tea and watched it cool while she rang Echo.

"Jenna?" Linda asked. "How are you, honey? When will you be back? Friday's the wedding, right?"

Wrong. She talked a few minutes to them both, hearing the pity in Linda's voice, and the concern in Olav's. "Give Goldfisch a pat for me," she said just before she hung up.

Huddled on the sofa, she tried to puzzle out how something so beautiful as her love for Simon could possibly have gone so wrong. She tried to reach him again that evening, and all day Friday, leaving her name and number with the service and waiting, waiting, waiting for his call.

The last of August was unbearably hot. Jenna thought wistfully of Little Bay Lake. She had received a letter from Megan and a snapshot of Beth holding her little brother. "We'll see you next summer for sure, all three of us," Megan had said.

That, at least, had come right. Beth would be going to school—first grade—in the fall.

Jenna found her father's copy of *Kenilworth* and finished reading it, and wept for Amy Robsart. She wondered if Simon had been back to the cottage and what he would think when he found the fisherman sweater she'd been knitting for him. She had almost finished it; there'd been just one more sleeve to do.

She fell asleep that night and dreamed of Simon and somehow her dream was all mixed up with the old fairy tale of the twelve princes who were turned into wild geese by a wicked stepmother and were able to return to human form only when their little sister knit sweaters for each of them. But the youngest prince got the sweater that lacked one sleeve, and Jenna awoke with tears on her cheeks.

182.

She sat in the kitchen, drinking coffee while dawn crept over the city. She was past pride now, and the ache was still as sharp as ever two weeks later.

When she dialed Simon's apartment, no one answered. The woman at the answering service reported that Dr. Andersen was now taking Dr. Fraser's calls and would she care to leave her number for the new physician?

So Simon had gone back to his north country! Jenna wondered if she dared telephone the cottage. She knew the number by heart. It was six thirty, and Simon would be up, walking to the kitchen door to let Goldfisch out . . .

Her fingers shook when she picked up the instrument, then she lost her nerve completely. For what was changed?

She left for work without breakfast again that day. An exasperated Daphne fretted about her and wondered if she perhaps ought to give Jenna the letter from Simon that she'd been carrying around in her handbag for two weeks.

The people at work worried about Jenna too. She was down one whole dress size by the middle of September and had to take in all her clothes.

That night she slipped on the beloved pink dress and stood in front of the mirror and stared at her reflection. This was how she would have looked for her wedding. But happy, though, not like this sad-eyed shadow of the earlier Jenna.

She fixed the seams in the mulberry suit and the jade-green dress and the basic black for herself. She wept quietly, tears running silently down her cheeks as she stitched.

Blake accused her of being a martyr. "Everything's working out okay," he shouted at her, "but you're making us all feel guilty as hell."

They were all trying too hard, he decided. Daphne was even helping a little with the housework. Toeing the line took all the fun out of life. When he and Jenna had the last of his gambling debt paid off, Blake intended to celebrate.

Jenna knew it wouldn't be so long now. She had marked the days off on her purse calendar. Just three more payments. Late October would see the last of the dreadful affair.

Blake's "biggies" had been perfectly willing to settle for Jenna's installment payments when she had marched into the club one night and demanded to see the man in charge. The tall, black-haired manager had asked Jenna for a date too, and with genuine regret watched her march straight out again, after they had arrived at a mutually agreeable mode of settlement. It was an arrangement he had never made before. And he saw to it from then on that Blake Wilson was not admitted to the private card room of the club.

In the last week of September Jenna's Great-uncle Wilson died at the age of ninety-one. He had been ill for many years. Jenna was happy that he was at peace, but she wept a little, too, for the kindly man who, in his eighties, had always looked forward to her visits.

Parker Hamilton called on them the Saturday afternoon following the funeral. Jenna had been surprised when he asked for the appointment, and Blake and Daphne were equally curious.

"Dear, now don't put too much drama into the announcement," Martha warned when she kissed her husband good-bye. Her gray eyes sparkled. "Oh, I should so like to be there."

Shrewd old Parker Hamilton had been the victor in many a courtroom battle, and he had planned this conference as carefully as any multimillion-dollar case. If all went as he expected—

The document he pulled from his briefcase was obviously a will. Blake's hopes rose. Who would have thought it of Great-uncle Wilson? The old boy certainly had been a sly one.

"I asked to see you three this afternoon, because I know you each are employed and this time would undoubtedly be the most convenient for you," he began.

"Decent of you," Blake murmured, wishing the old man would get on with the business. He did a little mental calculation. If Great-uncle Wilson had had his money in even a simple savings account for twenty-six years at, say, an average of three percent—though of course the nursing home would have cost a packet too—Maybe the old codger had had some real estate? Jenna probably knew; she'd gone down to see him often enough.

Mr. Hamilton was saying," . . . And it hasn't taken much acuity to see things weren't going just right for you three, and naturally I've been afraid it was concerned with money, so here I am, feeling a bit like an aging *deus ex machina*, coming to you today with some news which may solve your difficulties."

He looked directly at Jenna as he spoke. Clearing his throat he began to read: " . . . and to my beloved grandniece Jennifer Anne Wilson, the sum of twenty thousand dollars and the residence at 17431 South Park Street, for her loving kindnesses to me over a period of many years."

"But—" began Jenna with a puzzled expression on her face. Mr. Hamilton frowned and said, "I suspect I know what you were going to say, my dear, but would you please wait to comment until I have completed the reading of the pertinent portions of the will and have opened the floor to comments and questions?"

Jenna swallowed hard and nodded.

"To my dear grandnephew Blake Wilson Junior I

185

leave my gold watch and a twenty-dollar bill, that being the size of his usual loan request, none of which was ever repaid.

"And to my dear grandniece Daphne Elvira Wilson I leave one hundred dollars, ample payment for the single duty visit paid me on the occasion of her graduation from elementary school."

Mr. Hamilton cleared his throat again. "There follow numerous small bequests to a number of his friends, most of whom predeceased your great-uncle by several years."

Blake said succinctly, "Twenty thousand bucks!"

Daphne laughed. "One hundred dollars won't even pay my dress bill this month." She saw Jenna's look of alarm and commented spitefully, "All right, so I charged a little. You should worry, you just inherited a mint."

Mr. Hamilton said smoothly, "In times like these, when one legatee enjoys so much larger a share than the less fortunate ones, I often recommend that the—uh—spirit of generosity prevail."

Blake nodded. "Well said." Bless the old boy—hardly legal, but a mighty welcome thought. "As a matter of fact," he said, "the money couldn't have come at a better time. It will be pure bliss to get some of my bills off my back."

"What bills?" Jenna demanded. "We made a three-way agreement to charge absolutely nothing for three months until . . . well, you know—"

Mr. Hamilton sat back in his chair with a satisfied feeling. So far everything was going just as he had planned.

Blake fished in his pocket. "I didn't know how to tell you, Jenna, but this seems as good a time as any, with Great-uncle's money to cushion the shock."

Jenna stared wildly at the small card he passed her.

"Personal—five hundred dollars. Blake, no!" She was horrified.

"I'm afraid so. A different place, of course. Unfortunately, my luck was no better than before. I'm a reformed character for sure this time. Or I will be when I get this one paid."

"Dear me," Parker Hamilton observed, "dress bills and—er—card debts, I presume. How fortunate that Jenna has this money to assist you both."

Daphne rejoiced, "Our austerity regime is over!"

"About that property," Blake said, assuming a more dignified tone, "am I remembering correctly—is that the brick home on the double corner lot?"

"Stop it!" Jenna cried out. "Stop it, all of you." She looked at her employer. "Tell them the truth. There's no will at all."

"Oh, on the contrary, my dear girl. There is indeed a will. This one, all duly drawn and witnessed by Hamilton, Redford and Jones before you came to work for me, Jenna. Unfortunately, however, your great-uncle's assets are all gone, expended over some eight years on medical care and nursing home expenses."

Daphne giggled. "What a lark! You mean he didn't have a bean to his name when he died?"

"Alas, no. Scarely enough to pay for his funeral. But I knew you three would have wanted to know his intentions, nevertheless."

Blake's lips were tightly drawn in barely controlled anger. But it was at Jenna that the old attorney was looking.

"You knew, didn't you, my dear?"

"Well, yes. You see I visited him a good deal, and even five years ago when Father was still alive, we were aware that nearly all his money was gone."

"And now what?" he asked her quietly.

187

"Yes," said Blake. "Now what?"

Jenna turned to him. "I'm sorry for you, Blake, but I can't help you. No one can, except yourself. I tried, and it was no use. Simon was right. I've given you and Daphne too much assistance, too much of me. I love you both and I always will, but I don't like either of you very much these days. My car keys please, Blake."

To Mr. Hamilton she said, "You're an old scoundrel and you know it. Give Martha my love—and thank you."

"Where are you going?" Daphne asked.

"Why, to Simon, naturally."

Once she had told Simon that she would pack in two seconds to come to the one she loved. It took her somewhat longer, but she was packed, showered, and in the pink dress and heeled sandals by three o'clock.

Blake had gone out and Jenna didn't much care. Daphne had stayed to kiss her good-bye, refusing to miss even one minute of this high drama. "But you're not wearing pink cotton *now*, are you? Not in the last week of September!"

"Yes, I am," Jenna laughed. "Bye, Daphne. You've got a lot going for you, honey. You'll be all right. Say good-bye to Blake for me. Oh, and give Don my best wishes."

She had one more thing to do before the old Dodge could head north. A promise to keep . . .

The discreet saleslady lifted her eyebrows slightly when Jenna came hurrying in. A lovely girl, and wearing a Greensleeves dress, but—pink cotton at this time of the fall?

"Is Madame in?"

Madame was in. Jenna twirled around for her, and the dress followed every lovely curve. "It's my wedding dress," Jenna said. "How do I look?"

"Delightful, my dear. Just as I knew you would."

Jenna told her, "Do you know what? If I had a bridesmaid, it would be you."

"I believe you," Madame replied. "Be happy, child."

By four o'clock Jenna had hit the Interstate and was on her way to Simon. It was a long trip for a girl alone, a girl who was still a little uneasy about driving. She drove rather slowly and stopped four times: twice for gas, once for coffee, and once to ease her feet out of the sandals and into her mocs.

She worried a bit about the dress; it was bound to get somewhat dirty, but she wanted to come to Simon in the pink dress. Her wedding dress. None other.

Ten hours later the old Dodge went through Minowac and turned northwest in Vilas County. First the hard-topped road, then onto the gravel one, and finally onto the last mile.

The car bumped along the uneven roughness of the dirt road and came to a jerky halt in the clearing before the cottage. She heard Goldfisch's excited barking and saw a light flash on in the bedroom. And then Simon was there on the little back stoop, tying the belt of his old white terrycloth robe about his waist and staring intently at her as she slipped on the sandals and scrambled, laughing, out of the driver's seat and started eagerly to him.

He did not move. Jenna realized suddenly that he was frowning.

"Simon?" Her laughter faded away in the night and she stood very still in the moonlit dark, weariness sweeping over her now.

She said dully, "Am I too late?"

Gravely the man studied her lovely face. "That depends," he answered warily.

All the way up from Chicago she had been telling herself that everything would come right once she

189

reached him, but now she felt tired and hopeless. "Depends on what?"

He shrugged. "On whether you mean 'too late tonight' or 'too late for you and me.' "

A storm of love clutched at her heart and she swayed a little, steadying herself with one hand on the car. Pale in the moonlight, her face turned up to his. "Simon, please—please don't let it be too late for us. I wore the wedding dress . . . "

He uttered a small, choked sound and moved swiftly, gathering her into the heartsease of his embrace, kissing her mouth with sudden fierceness. "Jenna—dear girl—dear woman—I've missed you so. Why didn't you answer my letter?"

She felt his arms, strong and firm, lift her up and hold her close to his heart. "What letter?" she asked him.

"It doesn't matter," he said urgently. "Listen, I love you. Whatever's wrong in your life, anywhere, we'll work it out together. I promise you, sweetheart, brave, brave girl, from this time forward there's only you—for always—for as long as I live."

His lips moved against her throat. "You're wearing the wedding dress, so when's the wedding?"

She touched his tense, white face with trembling fingers. "As soon as ever we can. Like tomorrow?"

Over his shoulder she could see the dawn stars shining above the tall pines now. Simon kissed her; his face was warm against her own. He reached for the door, elbowing it open while she rested her head against his chest.

"Tomorrow's already today," Simon said, looking at the kitchen clock. "Welcome home, love."

Dell Bestsellers

- [ ] TO LOVE AGAIN by Danielle Steel $2.50 (18631-5)
- [ ] SECOND GENERATION by Howard Fast $2.75 (17892-4)
- [ ] EVERGREEN by Belva Plain $2.75 (13294-0)
- [ ] AMERICAN CAESAR by William Manchester ... $3.50 (10413-0)
- [ ] THERE SHOULD HAVE BEEN CASTLES
  by Herman Raucher $2.75 (18500-9)
- [ ] THE FAR ARENA by Richard Ben Sapir $2.75 (12671-1)
- [ ] THE SAVIOR by Marvin Werlin and Mark Werlin . $2.75 (17748-0)
- [ ] SUMMER'S END by Danielle Steel $2.50 (18418-5)
- [ ] SHARKY'S MACHINE by William Diehl $2.50 (18292-1)
- [ ] DOWNRIVER by Peter Collier $2.75 (11830-1)
- [ ] CRY FOR THE STRANGERS by John Saul $2.50 (11869-7)
- [ ] BITTER EDEN by Sharon Salvato $2.75 (10771-7)
- [ ] WILD TIMES by Brian Garfield $2.50 (19457-1)
- [ ] 1407 BROADWAY by Joel Gross $2.50 (12819-6)
- [ ] A SPARROW FALLS by Wilbur Smith $2.75 (17707-3)
- [ ] FOR LOVE AND HONOR by Antonia Van-Loon .. $2.50 (12574-X)
- [ ] COLD IS THE SEA by Edward L. Beach $2.50 (11045-9)
- [ ] TROCADERO by Leslie Waller $2.50 (18613-7)
- [ ] THE BURNING LAND by Emma Drummond $2.50 (10274-X)
- [ ] HOUSE OF GOD by Samuel Shem, M.D. $2.50 (13371-8)
- [ ] SMALL TOWN by Sloan Wilson $2.50 (17474-0)

At your local bookstore or use this handy coupon for ordering:

| Dell | DELL BOOKS
P.O. BOX 1000, PINEBROOK, N.J. 07058 |

Please send me the books I have checked above. I am enclosing $_____
(please add 75¢ per copy to cover postage and handling). Send check or money
order—no cash or C.O.D.'s. Please allow up to 8 weeks for shipment.

Mr/Mrs/Miss _____

Address _____

City _____ State/Zip _____

Love—the way you want it!

Candlelight Romances